NOT BURIED
DEEP ENOUGH

A Collection of Dark Matters

by Gary Robbe

Denver Horror Collective

Praise for
NOT BURIED DEEP ENOUGH

"In reading Gary Robbe's highly compelling NOT BURIED DEEP ENOUGH, it occurred to me the best horror fiction is not about the verbs, but the adjectives. Action is important, certainly, but anyone can write about the monster emerging from beneath the bed. Robbe's brilliance is in telling you what that monster looks like. Smells like. And the precise sound its mouth makes as it begins to bite into your flesh. The stories in this collection are all superb examples of visceral imagery paired with dread, so much so I believe my stomach was clenched the entire read. Bravo, Mr. Robbe, you scared the hell out of me."

Carter Wilson, *USA Today* bestselling author of *Mister Tender's Girl*

"Not Buried Deep Enough is filled with new ideas that are horrifically wonderful. All of the stories are whip-smart, creepy, and masterfully plotted. I highly recommend it."

Jeani Rector, Editor of *The Horror Zine*

"Robbe takes you from the WWI Western Front to suburbia to Little Bighorn and finds every nook and cranny of horror along the way. Deft characterization and Robbe's clear voice guide you through a roller coaster of stories sure to please the horror lover in all of us."

Sam W. Anderson, author of *Slightly Off-Center* and *The Money Run*

"Manifesting terror through exquisite characterization is the domain of horror masters only. Gary Robbe executes this technique flawlessly in his debut collection. Readers beware: a lingering sense of dread will follow you long after you've turned the last page."

Todd Sullivan, author of the fantasy series
The Windshine Chronicles and the *Vampire Series of Extreme Horror*

"Not Buried Deep Enough is a collection that is at once classic and experimental. Robbe deftly conquers westerns, war, ghosts, aliens, and much more, twisting and combining classic tropes to deliver truly unique tales that examine what death takes and leaves behind. These dark stories will bury their hooks deep and haunt you long after you're done."

Angela Sylvaine, author of *Frost Bite* and *The Dead Spot*

"An outstanding collection of short fiction from a master storyteller. This twisted collection of macabre delights will have any horror fan flipping pages long past the witching hour."

Travis Heermann, author of *The Ronin Trilogy* and the *Shinjuku Shadows* series

Denver Horror Collective
Denver, Colorado

NOT BURIED DEEP ENOUGH
Copyright © 2023 by Denver Horror Collective.

Cover design, layout, and graphics by Michael Picco.

PRINT:
979-8-9887639-0-1

EBOOK:
979-8-9887639-1-8

Printed in the United States of America

For Zak and Alex

Table of Contents

Acknowledgements

Many thanks to the following:

Josh Schlossberg, a superb writer and editor, and a major force behind Denver Horror Collective. This collection would not have come about without him.

Denver Horror Collective, for providing invaluable support and comradery over the years. An incredibly talented group of people.

The Colorado Chapter of the Horror Writers Association, for accepting me into their ranks when I moved to Colorado.

The editors of all the magazines, e-zines, anthologies, and podcasts who have accepted and published my stories.

The *Bewildering Stories* team—a fantastic group of people I've had the pleasure to work with over the years.

Michael Picco for his excellent cover and layout.

Thomas C. Mavroudis for the flattering foreword and Zak Hennessey for his meticulous proofreads.

Maria, for your friendship and unwavering support.

And a special, heartfelt thanks to all the readers out there who have shared my journey as a writer.

Introduction

by Thomas C. Mavroudis

Sometimes, things just stick with you. Not everyone, just you. In your own little personal sphere, the one you occupy alone, legends are made, truths are cemented, and you can't shake them, no matter what the exterior of your world suggests or proves.

Despite this acknowledgement, every time I read a story by Gary Robbe that does not refer to a snake on the ceiling at some point, I am little dismayed, and I don't hesitate to tell him so. The truth is, of all the work by Gary I've read, only one has snakes on the ceiling. Yet in my mind, I really think there must be several.

Since Gary has been producing fiction much longer than I have known him (through Denver Horror Collective's writing critique group), and therefore I have not read the substantially large output by the man, I thought I should prepare for this introduction with a little test to see how many snakes—on the ceiling or otherwise—are actually in this collection. And the conclusion was as I knew deep in my heart it would be: Gary has so many more horrors writhing around in his brain than snakes.

Here is what I do know about Gary Robbe. He is soft-spoken. He is educated, well-read, and he loves history. He has a great appreciation for all genres of music. He is always sending books to his son. In the best possible way, he is one of those stereotypical Midwesterners: true salt of the Earth. Honest and genuinely kind, Gary doesn't pose. And his fiction doesn't pull any punches. Behind his easy-going cheerfulness lies an imagination wrought with fear and despair. That's why we read him. That's why he deserves to be read.

Spanning time and space, Gary's work is indicative of who he is, who most of us are. His characters are everyday men, women, and children, recognizable folks befallen by the worst events of their lives...and often, their deaths. It's what resonates in the best horror fiction, the undeniable connections, the glimpse at what could happen to you or me at any given moment.

What else do I know about Gary? I'm going to let you learn from the man himself. I've never been interested in behind-the-scenes contents of movies—to me, it decays so much of the visual magic. But I love hearing about where an author's stories come from, and in NOT BURIED DEEP ENOUGH Gary has provided a little insight into each of his tales.

Unfortunately, there is not one mention about his relentless obsession with snakes on the ceiling. Maybe one day, when I write Gary's biography, I'll get to the root of it.

Foreword

by Gary Robbe

Thirteen stories. Thirteen stories originally buried somewhere in my brain, just not buried deep enough.

I've always agreed with Stephen King that stories are found, like fossils, dug out neatly or not so neatly, dusted and polished and then presented to the world. Sometimes, in the chiseling process, pieces of the fossil are broken off or dulled with the polishing, but the end result is still something discovered and dug out from the mind, regardless of the final condition.

Some of the stories in this collection took a long time to dig out and prepare, especially ones that required a great deal of research. Some stories took a lot of time to write and needed multiple rewrites. And there were a few that screamed to be freed and were written fast and effortlessly, as if I were possessed by some long dead author.

I've been writing off and on for over fifty years. I could have more stories written and published than I do, but my family and a career in education were always higher priorities. I have zero regrets about my choices.

I began submitting stories to various magazines and anthologies in the late seventies and early eighties. The days of SASE's (self-addressed stamped envelopes). I aimed high and received nothing but form rejections at first, then at some point I graduated to personalized rejections. A few well-known editors even offered brief critiques and suggestions along with encouraging words.

In the early eighties I fell in with a disreputable group of people connected with television, and I managed to do some writing for local cable shows (this was when the cable industry was in its infancy). I also wrote a screenplay for an experimental movie produced for cable television and met with several other writers on a weekly basis to churn out television scripts for shows like *Tales from the Darkside* and *The Twilight Zone*.

We never made a sale but came close enough to receive encouraging words from the producers. One short screenplay resurfaced within the past three years and was rewritten by one of our little group into a full-length independent movie screenplay. That movie (titled, *George – A Christmas Fable*) finished production in 2022 and will be released in December 2023.

In 2005 I wrote a crime novel which, after a rewrite, became a comedy-crime novel, then after a few years' time a horror novel. It's destined to be one of those works that likely will never be finished, but that's okay—it's been great practice. And it got me back into the writing game.

As my children became older and I got closer to retirement, I devoted more time to writing and submitting short stories. I received rejections, of course, but also enough acceptances to keep going. I primarily wrote crime and horror fiction, sometimes science fiction and literary. They are almost all dark. I can't explain why, but they are.

Most of these stories in *Not Buried Deep Enough* have been published before. There are three western horror stories. One vampire story. One horror/science fiction story. Two haunted house stories. One World War I story. One pulp zombie (maybe) story. And three attempts at literary/experimental. The science fiction one was written in the early eighties, forgotten about, then lengthened and fleshed out many years later. The others were written and published in the past ten years.

My hope is that you enjoy reading some of these stories as much as I enjoyed writing them.

Sincerely,
Gary Robbe

The Flesh You Break

Originally published by NoSleep Podcast Season 19, Episode 10, 2023

Maam's eyes were dark hollow patches when we took the wet poultice cloths off, like the eyes wanted to go with the filthy rags and not stay with her head. She moaned and shifted in the bed and tried to open at least one eye in the dismal cabin light. Bell and I looked at each other. His hand shook bad, and he dropped the snot green slime rags on the bed beside Maam before wiping his hand on his trousers the way he always did after sneezing into it. I slipped past him to lift the sheet just a little to see if there was any change, trying hard not to gag with the stench that drifted out.

I've smelled death before. Pa lingered for weeks with consumption smelling of it, coughing and spitting his bloody insides out. He suffered terribly, but the son of a bitch deserved it. I wish he could've suffered a few weeks more. The smell was with him to the end. That was two years ago, about.

And then there was Roust. I had to put the poor dog down after his run in with a bear that left him split open head to tail. He was beyond whimpering with a vacant desperate look in his eyes, lifting what was left of his head to the muzzle of the .22, like, *Get it over with, Cal.* It was the hardest thing I ever did, pulling the trigger with him looking at me like that.

Pa made me do it, handed me the gun and said be a man. "If ya ain't, then I'll make one outta you, and you still gonna put that mangy pup outta his miseries." I enlisted Bell to help dig a hole by the creek where the ground was easy and soft to move, and we buried Roust there. Next year a flood carried off the remains, and I wished we'd buried him higher up the bank.

Pa was proud I done it and didn't beat me for a whole two weeks.

Through the window I saw the dilapidated outhouse rising from the bottom fog and just beyond it, thick woods with a slow creek running through it. The woods belonged to Ley, who made it his home most of the time.

He was the oldest of us, the one missing something in his head, the something that sets us apart from the animals. He would come around sometimes like a suspicious mongrel, eager to take scraps of food and news but weary of getting too close. Ley left home shortly before Pa got sick and never came back until Pa was buried deep enough to make him confident Pa couldn't dig himself out. He came around more often with Maam dying. Likely the smell of death drew him. I stared out the window and waited for Ley to come loping out from the woods, but all I saw was flying leaves and dust.

It was late afternoon. Dark clouds moved in and fitted between the dark tree branches that hung from the dead oak next to the cabin like burnt crisp puzzle pieces. We expected it to rain bad.

Maylyn came in the room and shuffled to Maam like she was approaching a scared, cornered polecat. She rested both hands on the curled sheets at the bottom of the bed and stared at the shivering thing masquerading as her momma. Maylyn hardly ever came in this room anymore. She was five years old, tall for her age but skinny as a green switch. She was the youngest. "Did you make the spell yet?" she whispered.

Maam jerked her hand. Maylyn jumped seeing such a thin twiglike apparition make a motion. She stepped back, but Bell moved in and nestled her closer.

"It's still Maam," he said.

Maylyn shook her head real slow, eyes burning into the figure lying in such a state, as if she could miraculously make it all go away. Hardly believing such a change in Maam in only a few days' time. Bell patted Maylyn on the shoulder and as his eyes drifted to the poultices, he swallowed hard and turned green.

"I don't want Maam to go away," Maylyn said.

"We won't lose Maam," I said. I locked eyes with Bell. He was younger than me by a few years but lightning sharp with most things, and he remembered most of what Maam taught us. Like how to capture spirits and send them somewheres else, or how to confuse death angels or devils when they come to take away someone you love. She taught Bell and me these things weeks ago, before her brain clouded and her body stiffened like one of those manikins you see in city stores.

I turned to Maylyn and tried my best to smile. Leaves rattled against the window and a draft slipped in from somewhere enough to chill all of us into goosebumps. "I'll fetch the water," I said and left the room. The spring was about a hundred yards south of the cabin. I filled two one-gallon jugs with water and brought them back to the kitchen. I still didn't see any sign of Ley.

When I came back to Maam's room, Bell was mumbling the hymn, "He Leadeth Me," which had been Maam's favorite before Pa took sick. After Pa was buried Maam stopped going to church altogether and would have nothing to do with any kind of religious talk or song. About this time, she was mostly in the company of Old Widow Spenser, who lived in the next holler all by herself and was reputed to be a witch. Maam said the poor thing was lonely, was all, and didn't understand why folks neglected her so much. Old Widow Spenser was old but didn't look like a witch—not to me anyways—she was tall and broad and quiet as a mouse, yet it was known she too had nothing to do with church or the town or anyone besides Maam.

Even though Old Widow Spenser didn't *look* like a witch, we avoided her like she was one, and were careful not to look her in the eyes when she came around to visit Maam. Old Widow Spenser died just before Maam's accident with the copperheads.

Bell must've thought his mumbling at a hymn would calm Maam in her suffering, but it didn't, and he stopped when I shook my head and touched his arm.

"Can't we do somethin'?" Bell asked. He was scrawny and sensitive to a fault. The worry had settled in his hands which always trembled like he was chilled to the bone.

"We promised not to do anything," I said. "She wanted it this way."

"She can't have wanted to suffer like this."

I've known of others in the county that got bit by copperheads, and they came out of it all right, but Maam got bit six, seven times and she'd been suffering bad the past few weeks. I knew she didn't expect God to heal her the way she turned her back on him after Pa died. Maybe she expected Old Widow Spenser to rise from the dead and put some healing spells on her— she never said. What Maam did say once, was that Old Widow Spenser *was* a witch. Of sorts. And she shared some of the secrets with me and Bell that the old woman had shared with her.

Early on Maam got all of us together, even Ley, and made us all swear not to interfere with what she was going through. "It has to be this way," she said, "and if I look like I'm dead, leave me be. I aim to come back, and I don't want to havta claw through six feet a dirt to do it."

Of course, we all agreed, especially since Maam wasn't so bad right at first, but it wasn't long after she took a turn and what used to be Maam became something else, something barely human. So much pain and fever twisted her brain and sent torrents of babble outta her mouth. But every once in a while she became Maam again, clear headed, still in pain, but Maam. And she would remind us of our promises.

Bell and I figured Old Widow Spenser put a spell of some kind on her, or something, and Maam knew that suffering was part of the deal if she was to come back. From the dead, I suspect.

We stood around the bed watching Maam, shadow sleep gestures fighting in the air. Then Becca came in the room after walking into town to cash Maam's social security check and pick up some things we needed. She looked like a bent willow after hauling a heavy sack of goods two hours in the hot Kentucky sun. Dust covered her legs, and her Sunday green dress was dusty too and wrinkled with sweat. Becca was the second oldest, fifteen, and though she and Maam were at each other all the time like hissing geese, it was clear she was taking this hard.

Becca was set to run off with Garland Wilson when Maam stumbled into a nest of copperheads while cleaning beneath the woodshed. Becca decided to wait until Maam got better, then decided to wait until Maam died, when things got worse.

Garland was a second cousin by way of Maam, and Maam didn't like him one bit. No way she was going to approve of the two of them moving off. The copperheads settled things. Garland said he'd wait, and once things resolved one way or the other, they would move to Atlanta. Becca was crazy sick of this place, but I guess she felt guilty leaving with Maam the way she was. Becca wasn't the prettiest girl in the county by a long shot, but she was probably the easiest for the boys to get to know, judging by how popular she was with all of them.

Garland had blinders on when he agreed to run off with her.

Maam gurgled, and Becca wiped her mouth, then placed a fresh washcloth on her forehead. Ley, finally, found his way into the cramped smelly room. He was muddy from the knees down and wore the biggest of the copperheads that killed Maam around his waist like a belt. Ley was several years older than Becca and had eyes that widened with terror whenever he was someplace with a roof over his head. He was skinnier than the rest of us and freckled mean like Pa, born to live wild and die wild.

"Maam?" Ley said, leaning over her, his voice a whisper carried on a twisted wind. Maam stirred some more. One eye opened and fluttered like it was about to fly away on its own. He said what the rest of us couldn't even begin to say. "There's a spot nexta' Pa for you to rest in once your suffrin' stops. I was out there today. The locus is spreadn' out over the top and'll shield you from the sun with those pretty blossoms." He smiled to show the few teeth he had left.

Maam's lips trembled out something resembling a word. She repeated it a little clearer. "Don't." She drifted off to where closed eyelids go.

Bell repeated, "Don't?"

Becca shifted over to me and took my hand, then let it go. She reached over and touched Maam's gray hair, and it was like an electric shock the way she suddenly jerked her hand back. The silence in that little room was unbearable.

Maam. Pa told me once she wanted to be called that 'cause she never got any respect when she was growing up. We called her Maam, and the folks in town called her Maam, but Pa never did that, I recall. Her given name was Leona. I only know that because I heard Pa say that name over and over whenever he gave her a beating.

Pa was as mean in sickness as he was in health, whether he drank or not, it didn't matter. He didn't have friends. He had a reputation for being quick tempered and eager to fight over the littlest things, and once he did fight, he let loose with all the meanness and fury that was stored up his whole soured life. Maam had said he could never be a happy man, and the closest I ever saw him to it was when I put Roust down.

We steered clear of him whenever possible. Maam certainly did although she had to give him what he needed a few times a month when he'd come home drunk from the tavern and drag her direct to the bedroom, regardless what anybody was doing. Listening to the slick animal grunts and curse words spilling out made us all uneasy and curious, and once or twice Bell slipped to the door in the dark to try to peek in. If he saw anything he never shared it with us.

Maam's eyes opened, all cloudy and stained, and we could tell she was as awake as she could be. She didn't moan or nothing, but I knew the pain was eating her up. She wasn't going to last much longer. Bell and I did say some of the words over her that Maam made us write down a week earlier, and we continued to give her the awful-smelling stuff in the mason jar that Old Widow Spenser gave her just before she died. Maam kept it hidden from us until the accident, then had Bell and me spoon some of the jelled mixture to her several times a day. We had to say the words when we did, some strange language that made my hairs stand on end when I spoke them out loud.

We couldn't get her to keep the foul potion down anymore, but we said the strange words just the same.

"Looks like the fever broke some," Bell said. Sweat rolled off Maam's forehead. Her paper-thin skin was wet and cool to the touch instead of blistering hot like the night before. Her legs were swollen beyond the sheets and black as night. She was dying despite the potion and the spells, and we all knew it.

Outside the wind blew through the trees and scratched some of the brittle branches against the roof. Maam twitched. She turned her head and looked at each of us in the room. "My babies," she whispered. She lingered in Ley's direction, Ley trying hard to grin and let her see the biggest of the snakes that killed her.

When Maam stumbled out of the shed with a couple of snakes tangled to her legs like writhing ropes, it was Ley who got to her first and tore them off her and cut their heads with a shovel. He wasn't afraid of snakes or any creature for that matter, but the look he gave us when we drug her into the house was one of hopeless terror. Maam was insistent we not fetch Doc Adams, or anyone.

"Leave me be," she said. And then she was delirious and in great agony, and some of the words she said made no sense, words that struck apart and couldn't be glued to other words in any fashion. "John," who was Pa to us. "Demon." "Hell." We were sure she was talking about Pa that way, knowing how much she hated and feared the man, but in strange moments she got clear headed and said the demons were in her, and Hell was her place if she died, for what she'd done.

In one clear moment she told Becca and me she killed the buzzard, with the Widow's help, and regretted none of it. The snakes somehow were a price she had to pay.

Something hit the window, and we all jumped, the wind fierce now, a storm blowing up. I noticed a crack in the yellow-gray glass. The trees bent and leaves flew everywhere. The sky, what we saw of it, a swirling midnight black. We don't get tornadoes in these hills, but even Ley said something was brewing bad, and it was easy to see relief on his face for being inside and warm.

Becca lit a kerosene lamp once the room was dark. Shadows lifted up immediately and danced across the ceiling. "What are we gonna do?" she asked.

"Nothing we can do," Bell said, looking at me. "We did the spells like Maam asked."

"It didn't do nothing for the Widow," Ley said, in one of his rare utterings.

Becca nodded in agreement.

"We don't know what the Widow did before she died," I said. "Likely she didn't have time to drink the potions, or maybe she just had enough of this world to not want to come back."

The kerosene lamp flickered. Maylyn ran into the kitchen and brought another lamp, already lit. Sweat glistened on all of us in the shadows even though the room was chillier than it ought to have been. Ley had a faraway look in his eyes. I imagined he thought about being back in the woods, or slipping into town to pick some fights, maybe spend a night or two in the constable's jail. It was always warm there.

Maam used to say that Ley was just like Pa, in many ways. Except he had a heart. And the sense to live away from people as much as possible. Ley avoided Pa like the plague most of his life, and when he dropped out of school at the age of twelve, he ran into the woods and never looked back. I remembered Ley always fighting back at Pa and taking beating after beating, until I guess he couldn't take it anymore. Ley was especially fond of Becca—maybe he blamed himself for what Pa used to do with her when Maam wasn't enough. I don't know.

Pa worked for the lumber company north of Albany over twenty years, and after he died Maam got a check from social security, fifty-seven dollars once a month, and that's what we lived on. Maam was too sick to sign the last check that came, so Becca forged her signature and cashed it for us. Becca was usually the one to walk the two hours to the bank in town since we don't have a car or even a mangy horse. Sometimes Bell and I went with her to help carry the food and supplies we needed. And once every while we were able to borrow old man Wilson's wagon, pulled by his gray sorrel Jubal, and that was a treat for everyone, Maylyn especially, going into town that way. Wilson's farm was a mile up from our little cabin on Hog's Bend Road, which wound past our holler on the way to Albany. When the sorrel Jubal died, we didn't see old man Wilson anymore.

No one in town knew Maam was sick. That's what she wanted, for no one to know. The townspeople all believed she was crazy anyhow, especially how she acted after Pa died and was buried in the church cemetery. She wanted him wrapped in a burlap sack and tossed in the Cumberland by the falls so the water would keep him down good and for all. But the lumber mill he worked at insisted he be buried proper in a cemetery with a Christian burial, even though Pa was nothing like a Christian and had never been in a church in his life.

Pa was placed in a remote overgrown section alongside Baby Catherine and Thomas Lee, who both died from whooping cough in different years, and it was a pretty site, like Ley suggested. If Maam had wanted it that way, we could have scraped up enough for a simple marker, and she would've had a nice view at least.

Maam struggled to the surface with a gasp, not unlike the smack against the window. "Don't nobody should know I'm dead," she said, like she had been in my head all along, reading my thoughts. "Don't want no service, that jackass preacher saying words that don't mean nothin'. Don't want y'all putting me in the ground, neither, and especially anywhere near that devil I was married to all those years…" She trailed off and swallowed at the air like a fish out of water, and we all rushed forward, all except Maylyn, who wasn't quite sure what this thing on the bed was attempting to say.

"Give me some air," Maam said, weakly, and we backed up some. "I'm not leaving my babies, no matter what, no matter what it looks like, no matter how long…" Maam closed her eyes, all the muscles in her gray sunken face relaxed and for the first time it looked like she was outta pain, at peace.

For what seemed forever we waited, until finally Ley said, "I'm not a baby, Maam." And he left and headed into the woods to be by himself, even with the rain still spitting about.

Maam moved her lips like she was trying to say something. I leaned over her, put my ear down near her mouth, the smell coming outta her something awful like she was already dead inside a long time. What I made out, what only I heard was, "I'm coming back."

—⁂—

Maam died that afternoon. The declining sun broke through what was left of the rain clouds and came across the opaque window and into the room, and we took it as a sign that Maam was right. She might look dead, and smell dead, but she was coming back like she said she would. We stood over her lifeless body all night.

Ley came back even before the sun was up, and it was like he knew what happened. He brought with him a necklace he fashioned from the copperheads' fangs, and he placed it reverently on Maam's bosom. No one said a word. No one cried like you would expect.

Everyone was bone tired. Becca went to the kitchen and came back with a wet cloth and a bucket, and she set about cleaning Maam best she could, the smell of dead fluids everywhere. The rest of us went into the kitchen.

"What're we gonna do?" Ley asked.

Becca came in and said, "She's dead, she don't care no more."

"We promised," I said. "We can't go back on our word."

"We promised someone who was alive. It ain't a promise no more when that person is dead. And besides, what's in that room ain't Maam anymore, and y'all know it. Maam's done gone up to heaven and don't give a lick what we do with that thing in there."

"She ain't gone nowhere," Bell murmured. "She's still in there." He paced the room, fists clenched. Bell rarely showed he was upset, rarely balled his fists. Runaway tears streamed down his cheeks.

"That's Maam in there, that's fer sure," Ley said. I don't think he quite got what Becca was talking about. Ley went and opened the door to Maam's room, peeked in. He lingered there and the unnatural odor of sick and decay drifted out. There is no hiding death.

Maylyn stayed by the kitchen window, next to me. We both looked through the doorway and saw Maam wrapped up mummy-style in sheets and her favorite Indian made star quilt. The window in that room was cracked open to let good air in and bad air out, as was the window by Maylyn and me. A warm breeze escaped from over the western hills.

Ley gasped.

"What?" I said.

He rushed into the room. We all followed. Ley stood by her bedside, the rest of us crowded just inside the door.

"She moved," he said in a hoarse voice. "I saw it." He unwrapped the sheet and quilt from Maam's face. One of the eyes was open, looking nowhere but open. We all saw it. I swallowed bile, and I suppose everyone else did, too.

Becca looked at me and nodded, and I went and felt for a pulse on her neck. The yellowish gray skin was cold and taut; I didn't feel a pulse. Becca ran to the kitchen and came back with a little mirror, which she put before Maam's closed blue lips. The mirror didn't fog up. Becca tried to close the eye, but the skin was tight and unyielding. She covered Maam's face with the quilt.

"She's dead," Becca said. She turned to Ley, who looked like he saw a ghost. "You must've been seeing things, Ley."

"I know what I saw."

Bell came next to me and pulled me aside. He whispered, "Maybe she's coming back, like she said she would, like she promised." He shifted around uneasy like he had to run to the outhouse.

I nodded. "Maybe." I'd heard stories from Luke Walters, the undertaker's son, about how sometimes corpses can twitch and move about, something to do with the muscles. Still, we did make Maam swallow that awful smelling stuff, and we said the strange words…

We couldn't talk in that room. I think we all suspected Maam, regardless her condition, could hear us and make judgment, so we went back to the kitchen.

"We got to do something," Becca said. "I don't believe those spells of the Widow's did anything." She glanced at Ley. "Not with the Widow dead and buried anyway."

"Maybe the Widow doesn't have to be alive for the magic to work, we don't know," I said. "If she was a witch, she coulda changed into something else before she died. She could be one of those fuckin' flies."

"Maam needs a burial. She needs the right words said over her."

"Hell, if she comes to and she's six feet under the ground," Ley said. He wandered about the room, unable to sit, like he couldn't finish the thought of Maam clawing at the inside of a wood box.

No one said a word after that.

—⚬—

The day dragged on. Everybody went about their chores, except Ley, who briefly disappeared into the woods. Becca made an oatmeal concoction that no one could keep down, Maylyn swept the place but only managed to move the dust from the floor to the air. Bell and I collected and chopped some wood for the fireplace, and we made many trips to the spring for water. We avoided Maam's room, knowing we would have to look in on her at some point, but we were in no hurry. If Maam decided to get up and move about while her door was closed, well, that was something none of us wanted to see. Not right now, anyway.

Ley brought a squirrel for dinner, and we ate that, and then we sat around the pine table and discussed things. Ley was wild but not dumb, and he made a good point about we might get in trouble if we told about Maam, now, weeks after she got bit, and we hadn't done anything about it. Becca saw the sense in that. We would be split up for sure. Becca might not get the chance to run off to Atlanta with Garland. Shy Maylyn would be put with strangers, alone. Who knew where Bell and I could wind up. We had no more family in these parts.

We shared Pa's whiskey that Maam always kept around for medicinal purposes, except for Maylyn, who had cider instead.

"We let her die," Bell said.

"We did what Maam wanted," I said.

Everyone stared at the table and the gnawed-over scraps of squirrel. It became dark, and the wind picked up again, rattling the door and windows. Several times while we sat around the table we heard knocks and creaking sounds coming from Maam's room, even something that sounded like foot-falls, but no one was eager to go check to see what they were.

"The window's open, remember?" Becca said, and that settled our minds some.

"What do you suppose happens when you die?" Bell asked.

"Go to heaven, I guess," I said.

"Naw," Ley said, "I think the lights just go out. Then you return to the earth the way everythin' does, where we come from to begin with."

"That don't make no sense, Ley," Bell said. "There's got to be more than everythin' just goin' black."

The rain started up again, and this time thunder railed through the holler along with flashes of light that illuminated our faces in the dark kitchen. We realized we had been sitting at that table like talking shadows with no faces. The lightning put our faces back on. I could see how scared everyone was.

Something hit Maam's door, hard, as if someone had thrown their body against it. We all junped from the table. Ley went to the door and put his hand on the doorknob and his ear against the wood. The flashes of lightning and the thunder increased, rain now pelting the roof and windows. We stood behind him, me, Becca, Bell, and little Maylyn, a chain of heartbeats, as Ley slowly turned the knob.

Foul wind, rich in musty decay, rushed through the widening crack. The room was pitch black except for flashes of lightning between the billowing curtains. And as we entered, we all felt the cool air and rain spray blowing through the window space, the glass shattered by what looked like a giant arm with gnarled fingers but was really a tree limb from the nearest tree.

Becca held a lamp toward Maam's bed. She was still on it, although somehow she had turned on her side facing away from the door. Maylyn screamed and ran into the kitchen. Bell went after her, while Becca and I turned Maam over on her back and once again checked to make sure she was dead. Ley pulled the branch into the room and kicked some of the bigger pieces of glass against the wall, out of the way of bare feet.

Maam was stiff and cool, and already the skin was turning a purplish-blue tint, except for her face with the open eye, which was pale and ashen. I knew she was dead, but beyond the wind whistling and the rain crashing against the house and shards of remaining glass, I heard a distant wailing somewhere outside, in or beyond the patch of woods. Ley heard it too, and he paused by the window and cocked his head in recognition.

Becca had already gone into the kitchen to find a piece of wood to nail over the window. Ley looked me in the eyes, terror frozen on his face. It wasn't the wail of an animal. It was the high-pitched cry of someone in great pain and grief, and it rippled through the rain and wind and rustle of trees the way a radio broadcast found its way past the static. His eyes said it all. The wailing, somehow, was Maam.

It was the same sound she'd made when she stumbled from the shed covered with copperheads. The same sound when she lost the babies. The wailing was not interrupted by thunder or the rush of blood in our heads. It was not human. It was *too* human.

The wailing faded as the storm moved on. Becca came in with a board, asked what was wrong, and we simply shook our heads, knowing she would think we were crazy. Knowing she would think we were afraid.

Ley nailed the board into the window frame. It would work well enough. Maam was recovered and seemed to be at peace. We closed the door and went to bed. Ley slept by the fireplace in the living room. Becca figured he didn't want to sleep in the wet woods.

I knew different.

During the night I left my room, which I shared with Bell, to go outside to use the outhouse. It was especially dark because the sliver of moon was covered in black rolling clouds, and even though a lamp was left burning in the kitchen it didn't shed any light from the curtained window. I was halfway there before my eyes adjusted to the darkness, and I could make out the peculiar likeness of every living and nonliving thing. I walked slow, my untied boots sucking the mud on the narrow path to the outhouse. No familiar night sounds came from the woods. No lonely birds, pesty insects, no scurrying twig scratching of rodents or larger animals moving about. In the absence of all other sounds, a sudden shriek or wail would be the worst terror to imagine.

I was wrong.

I finished my business quick as I could, then swung the outhouse door open to leave. Old Widow Spenser stood there, blocking the door, her features unmistakable even though most of the skin had been flayed off the bone. I fell back onto the toilet, flailing my arms before me in panic shock, the creature unmoving in the doorway, mouth clattering open and shut like it was trying to say something. Something moved along the corner of the mouth, a worm perhaps, and in the dark shadows it gave the appearance of a twisted smile.

I turned my head and squeezed my eyes shut, and once the air was allowed into my lungs I croaked, "Go away ghost!"

But she wasn't a ghost, at least not the kind of ghost I had ever heard of.

She was as solid, as real, as any corpse would be fresh dug from the grave. I huddled into myself, expecting to die.

"Cal?" It was Ley, calling from the cabin. I opened my eyes, and Old Widow Spenser was gone. But the smell remained, a three-day-in-heat rotting smell of something dead, blending and overpowering the shit, lime, sawdust smell of the pit. I ran to the cabin and met Ley on the front stoop.

"Did you see her?" I asked, out of breath.

"See who?" I saw in his eyes he was thinking of Maam, but he would never say that.

"Old Widow Spenser, dead as anything, standing right over there!" I pointed to the shadow outline of the dilapidated outhouse.

He shook his head. "Nothin' there, Cal, not when I come out, anyways. Mebbe you seen a bear, or big coon, somethin' like that. 'Sides, it's awful dark." He said the words, but I could tell by the tone he believed I *did* see the Widow.

I was shaking. Inside, we sat at the table and drank what was left of the whiskey. Maylyn came in and said she heard a scratching sound, and Becca joined us a few minutes later.

"You playing tricks? You tryin' to scare us?" she said to Ley and me. We shook our heads, no. Then she saw how upset I must've looked. "You look like you saw a ghost, Cal."

"I did." I told her about Old Widow Spenser, leaving out the gruesome appearance due to Maylyn being right there. Bell slipped in the room quiet as a mouse and sat at the table. It was the middle of the night, but nobody was going to take a chance on sleeping. Not 'til we sorted things out.

"You think Maam's going to come back like that Widow woman?" Becca believed what I saw. The thought of Maam looking like what I encountered by the outhouse made me ill. I nodded yes, then ran outside to vomit up every bit of squirrel and whiskey I'd had earlier. After I came back in and sat down, she asked, "When?"

"Don't know. Tomorrow. The next day, the day after that, hell..."

"Nobody knows Maam died," Bell said. We all nodded, even Maylyn, who looked like a porcelain doll, the way the lamplight eased and shimmered on her face. But still I could tell the thought was in everyone's mind, *What now?*

Then Bell said something that stopped everything right then and there. "She might be dead. She might not be. I think she's somethin' in between." His eyes locked with mine. "We made Maam drink the concoction the Old Widow gave us. We said the funny words over her. This is our fault. All of it." What Bell said next was the most chilling part yet. "And Maam kilt Pa, we all know it, she even said as much. It's why she's stuck in between. She's not dead. She's not alive. Cause of what we done. And what she done."

"We can't just leave her there, like that." Ley was agitated, pacing. The walls of the cabin too much for him, but the thought of being out there, in the dark, where Old Widow Spenser might be…

"We don't have a choice," I said. I went to Maam's door.

"Don't," Becca said.

"We got to see." I opened the door.

Darkness spilled out, specks of light from the lit lanterns in the kitchen spilled in. Bell carried a lantern and joined me just inside the room. We closed the door to keep the smell from drifting into the kitchen. Shadows flickered across Maam but she was as we last saw her, wrapped tight on the bed. Bell moved the lantern side to side, and both of us went to the bed and stood over Maam. Already there were flies, and they flew about our faces and lit on our skin.

"She ain't moved yet," Bell whispered.

While he was by the bed, I checked everything around the room to make sure there were no critters that had gotten in somehow. Maylyn said she had heard some scratching. The window, where it was boarded up, was secure. I peeked under the bed. Then I checked the inside of the door.

Scratch marks. Many of them, as if someone, or something, with long hard nails had been desperately trying to get out. Bell's breathing turned a shivering series of gasps. We looked back to Maam, and I know what he was thinking, *No way we were going to unwrap those sheets and quilt to inspect Maam's fingers and nails.*

"Don't say a word about this, you hear?" I whispered.

He nodded.

When we closed the door behind us, we told the others there was nothing in the room but Maam, and she was still where she was supposed to be, and still dead.

It was the longest night, all of us sitting up until dawn broke, deciding what we had to do, and the miseries attached.

—⁓—

That night we knew Maam had to stay where she was. Becca said we had to think practical. If people found out she was dead she would be buried for sure, and then what? We all remembered what Ley suggested about Maam waking up in the coffin six feet under. And the scratch marks on the door were forever etched on my mind. If Maam were to wander, better in her own room than a tiny pine box.

People would split what was left of the family, too. Becca might not be able to escape to Atlanta with Garland. Ley would be taken outta the woods, probably be put behind bars 'cause of his wildness. That would kill him. Maylyn was so little it might not matter much, but the thought of her alone somewhere missing everyone was unbearable. And Bell and me, who knows?

We didn't tell a soul. We swore ourselves to secrecy. Becca didn't even tell Garland. Maylyn didn't understand, but after a while she got used to Maam's room always being closed off. She cried all the time and stopped talking. But I think she knew Maam was going to come back some day, and that helped.

We all believed that.

Bell continued with school. I dropped out and took a job in town at the gas station. Once a month Becca wrote Maam's name on the check that came and cashed it. After Becca left with Garland a year later, Bell and I took turns writing Maam's name and cashing the checks at the bank. Everyone in town knew Maam was ill and asked about her whenever they saw any of us. We always said Maam was too stubborn to die, and as soon as she felt fit enough, she would come into town and say hello.

Ley didn't come around much anymore. When he did, he often brought meat from something he killed recent, and we would cook it up and visit. Ley refused to come into the cabin, so we talked and ate outside, regardless the weather. The last time I saw him he could barely look us in the eye, his dirt rash skin splitting out of his ragged clothes. The snakeskin belt still there, loose about his waist.

For a long while we slept on the porch at night because of the smell and the flies that somehow managed to get out of the room. Eventually the smell and the flies weren't too bad, and by the time it was winter that year we could sleep inside the cabin again. When Becca left, Bell, Maylyn, and me slept in the same room, and always had lanterns lit in the kitchen.

—⁓—

A year after Becca left Bell asked me what I thought, was Maam ever going to come back? How could we know if she did?

"Don't know," I said. I tried to picture what she looked like the last time I saw her, when I checked her pulse so long ago. I shuddered to think what she looked like now. "We don't know what those potions might a done. Maybe she came back as something else, and we just didn't know it." I thought of the many flies I had killed the past year. The critters Ley brought to eat. I think Bell was thinking the same thing.

We were both silent for a while. We sat on the porch smoking pipes and watching the orange sun set into the trees. Maylyn skittered around in the kitchen. She was almost eight now, in school, but she was different from the other children. She never talked, and she preferred to be by herself. She never caused any trouble though, and Bell and me knew she would never say anything about Maam. The teacher knew Maam was too ill to come to school meetings, so it was only natural that me or Bell did what talking or meeting needed to be done. No one ever came by the cabin to visit.

Maylyn came out and sat behind us on the porch steps. She had a drawing pad, and she was working on something, a picture she would never share with us. Maylyn drew hundreds of pictures, but never allowed anyone to see them, except Maam. She slipped them under the door each day. I expected the floor in Maam's room was knee deep in Maylyn's pictures by now.

"Maybe she *is* something different," Bell said. "You think she really done it?"

"What?"

"Killed Pa. Poisoned the son of a bitch. It's why he suffered so much in the end. Maybe that explains why the potion and the spells didn't work right, why Maam hasn't come back the way she's supposed to."

"Hell," I said. "You been thinkin' on that all this while?" I grinned. "I don't think what she did to that wretched man makes a difference one way or the other. Maam's still coming back." I said it loud enough for Maylyn to stop her drawing and stare off into whatever was beyond the woods.

Bell and me both knew what Maylyn was thinking. The same things we thought in the quiet times. We have heard things coming from Maam's room, from soft moans to shuffling footsteps, things lifted and set down, knocks and scratches at the door and boarded window.

Once I heard my name. But it could have been an ailing crow.

"How long you gonna stay?" Bell asked.

The tiny yard before us was littered with trash and spent tools long rusted, the woodshed to the side of the cabin twisted and ready to fall with the next big wind, and the dismal gray and blue woods crept closer to the cabin each year and made the distance to town seem further and further. I noticed the birds and crickets and all the squirmy things that bubbled noise on a midsummer day were silent and have always been silent.

"Don't reckon I have anywhere to go." I turned and looked at Maylyn, back to scribbling in her drawing pad, her face as clear of emotion as the creek running across slick mossy rocks.

Bell picked up a stone and tossed it across the yard into an old bucket with a clang. A smile swept over his face. "Yeah, me neither."

Maylyn stood and stared at what she had drawn. She sniffled, then carefully removed the paper from the drawing pad and held it to her heart. Maam was going to love it.

"The Flesh You Break" is a line from one of Dylan Thomas' poems. It always stuck with me, and as is often the case, I knew it would be a title for a story someday. That day came when I decided to try writing a story with an Appalachian setting, specifically southern Kentucky where my family on my mother's side had lived since the late 1700s. An image of a single parent dying in an isolated cabin and the dilemma the surviving children faced about what to do with the body came to mind.

Scrape

Originally published in Denver Horror Collective's Terror at 5280', 2019

An ever-present fog surrounds the house. I press my face and hands against the cool glass of the bedroom window, trying to see if there is any movement or sign of life within any holes in the mist. Disjointed memories flash inside my head. I have no control over them, when they come or how long they last. I don't know which ones are real or not.

—⁂—

The old house is being demolished. Mom, Dad, Rachel, and me standing by the curb on Downing Street watching the bulldozer close in for the first ceremonial punch to the bricks and wood structure. I like the two-story house. It has many rooms, nooks and crannies, places to explore and hide, overwhelming smells of must and caked dust, hints of decay. It is extraordinarily empty. A perfect place for an eleven-year-old boy.

But Mom and Dad have other ideas. The house will come down, and a new house will go up in its place. They only bought the house for the desirable land in a desirable neighborhood.

It's a hot summer day, no clouds in the sky, and although there are many trees on the street, all the ones on our property have already been taken down. The sun gleams off the yellow tractor until a plume of black smoke covers it. Dad coughs. Mom laughs. Rachel picks dandelions. I turn my attention to the house.

The reflection of dark cloud crosses the second story window. But it's not a cloud. Something is moving inside the house. I glance around to be sure. No planes, birds, giant insects, nothing. Maybe it's an optical illusion or possibly a couple of workers doing their last-minute preps inside before the bulldozer makes contact.

I return to the window. And I see a figure—no, figures—in the window. The figures are small, children, I guess, and I can barely make out faces resembling a boy and girl. Standing behind the window with the light hitting it makes them seem transparent. Unreal. The boy raises his hand.

I scream. That catches the attention of Dad, who quickly motions for the bulldozer to stop.

I shout over the rumbling idling engine. "There's somebody in there!" Then point to where I can see the vague but undeniably human faces behind the glare streaking across the window.

Dad looks that way and squints. "I don't see anything." He walks to the bulldozer where several workers mill about, says something to them, and all of them go into the house. I keep my eyes on the window until Dad appears, waving with a big grin on his face. Of course the house is dead empty.

—∞—

Six months later we are in our new house, a two-story box with transplanted trees and a rooftop deck. I can't remember a thing about the construction. We are simply here, inside, looking out new windows with the stickers still on them. All the furniture is new. It smells like a new house.

But that memory of the new house is brief.

I scratch the peeling window frame and wait for more holes in the fog to appear.

—∞—

Dad screams downstairs. He has found Mom. He knows he is the one who stuffed her in the fireplace. A window of sanity open for only a few moments, long enough for him to anguish and tear at his eyes and pound up the stairs to look for Rachel and me. He won't come into our rooms, he *can't* come into our rooms. The house stops him from that.

Is this happening now, or is this just another too-real memory slice? I close my eyes. I see Dad beneath the kitchen table, his head bashed in, Mom sitting down calm as can be with an empty cup before her as if she is pretending to have tea. A broken baseball bat on the floor next to her. When she looks up to us with those eyes that don't belong to her, Rachel and I run up the stairs to our rooms.

—∞—

Eyes closed or open, it doesn't matter. When a dream memory comes, I am there and it is real, however discordant or *wrong* it may seem. I imagine time means nothing. I imagine there are multiple versions of me across all kinds of planes of existence. I am twelve. I am thirty-five. I am dead. I was never alive.

Did I grow up in the new house, leave for college, meet a sweet girl I fell in love with, marry and have kids, two of them, Delilah and Matthew? I have memories of those things, but I have never left this house, never once made it past the desolate yard and the fog that surrounds us.

Every now and then when I stand at the window I see glimpses of what might be the real world in the holes of the fog, and in between the memories I think there is a chance to escape and maybe meet me on the other side.

—⚹—

The first night in the new house. Everyone is excited, especially Dad, who sees this as his finished project. Mom is everywhere at once, smiling and dancing and singing like she is on a honeymoon cruise.

Mom opens my closet door a dozen times. "I can't believe how much room you have in here."

"It's not that big," I say. It's just a normal step-in step-out closet with a bar to hang clothes and a couple of wire shelves. Mom makes a big deal out of everything.

Then she disappears into the closet, closing the door, the room becoming very quiet as if she stepped into another world. She pops out like she is playing jack in the box entertaining a two-year-old.

"Mom, stop. I'm not a baby."

Later, I look in the closet. It seems much smaller than before. I can't figure out how Mom, who is a big woman, could even fit in it. There's a musty smell too, something I hadn't noticed before. It reminds me of the original house that had been scraped to make room for this one. I step inside. Nothing strange. Boxes stacked to my chin, a few shirts and pants hanging on the wooden rod. Wait. The rod is supposed to be metal, not wood. And the wire shelves are gone, replaced by well-worn wooden ones. This is the closet I popped into before the house was scraped. The house that is gone. Gone.

The door swings shut. Everything is pitch black.

"Damn it, Rachel!" I yell. I push the door, but something pushes back, something stronger than me. "Mom? Dad?" Whoever it is stays silent. Then, a faint scratching, starting at the bottom of the door, moving upward and getting louder. The scratching grows in intensity, as whatever it is digs its nails into the wood of the door. I back away, expecting to stumble into the boxes.

I don't.

I swing my arms around in panic. It's not a closet anymore. What I am in is immense, my voice echoes as if I'm in a deep cavern. I run, but I'm not sure I'm running. I can't see. And I can't feel my feet strike the floor.

There is no memory of getting out.

—ɷ—

"Do we know anything about the people who lived in the house?" Mom directs this at Dad, who is busy rolling spaghetti around his fork. It's taking all his concentration.

"What?" The question sinks in. "An old couple, I think, lived there for thirty or so years. Don't know anything about anyone before them. The house is a hundred years old." He lights up, as if proud to tear down something that old.

"I like it the way it is," I say.

"It does have character," Mom says.

"Ha!" Dad scoffs. "Character means it's a money pit. Besides, everyone is doing this in Denver. Tearing down old wrecks and putting up new homes. Half the homes in Platt Park are scrapes. We'll save money in the long run."

"I'd rather stay where we are," I say. "All my friends are here." We are living in an apartment in Golden. My school is in Golden. My friends are in Golden. I don't want to be far away in Denver, having to make new friends all over again. The thought of being in a new school makes me sick.

"Tomorrow's the big day," Dad says.

Rachel, wearing her spaghetti-like mod jewelry, says, "What about the kids who live in the house?"

"No one lives there, honey," Mom says. "It's our house now. It's been empty for years."

"I've seen them," Rachel says. "A little boy and girl. They play hide and seek."

Dad laughs. "Nobody's there. Maybe some of the kids in the neighborhood sneak in—damn dangerous thing to do. And Mom and I have always been there when you kids were there. We never saw or heard anything. Come on, eat, forget this nonsense. When the new house is built you'll forget there ever was an old house on that spot."

—ɷ—

In my new bed, in the new house, unable to sleep, staring at the ceiling. Faint light from the moon filters in through the curtains, enough to make out multiple stains, cracks, and plaster folds in the ceiling. I imagine the stains and cracks taking on the shapes of snakes. I count them. Somewhere in the back of my mind there is an unsettling awareness that this is not the fresh smooth ceiling of a new house.

Two, three, four, a boa constrictor, there a western diamondback, coiled, big snakes, small snakes, seven, eight, nine…The diamondback uncoils. It slides effortlessly into a confluence of tangled snakes, all of them quivering and moving, bubbling from the ceiling as if about to drop.

I curl under a ball of sheets and covers, and a squeal escapes from my mouth. No one hears it.

—∽—

Dad stands at the front door with his briefcase in hand looking befuddled, as if he can't understand why he's there. Mom comes from the kitchen and asks why he hasn't left yet, is everything all right? He tries to form words, but nothing comes out, the hand on the doorknob moving to his hair as if to figure things out. Mom tells Rachel and me to go upstairs and get ready for school.

The next thing, I'm in my room looking out my window, fog coating everything, and it's getting dark.

—∽—

Mom stares at the ceilings and the peeling wallpaper, wallpaper that doesn't belong here in our new house. We are all in the living room, except for Dad, who hasn't moved from his bed in a long time. Mom spins, slowly, counting the stains and cracks and the plaster bubbles, trying to convince herself that simple arithmetic will change everything back.

Her eyes grow wide and wild when I tell her about the snakes on my ceiling coming alive. She has seen them, too.

—∽—

Rachel sees and hears the children all the time. She tells me about it but won't say anything about it to Mom and Dad because she knows they'll get mad. The children hide under her bed and in her closet, which is pretty small. She hears them playing inside her walls.

"That's impossible," I say. But deep down I know it's possible. This is not the same house anymore, the one Dad and the architects designed, the one we are supposed to be living in. None of us can even remember what that house looks like anymore. We've never seen it once we walked through the front door.

"They're here and can't get out," Rachel says. "Like us."

I don't say anything, I see a faraway spark of fear in her eyes, the eyes now of a much older girl. Somehow, we are holding on. How long have we been here? A few days? A week? Months? Everything is a blur to me, and I'm sure it's the same for Rachel. Mornings we get up and get ready for school, but that's as far as we go. Sometimes I am suddenly in the cold black closet that seems to go on forever. Or the living room, staring at a bloody mess of human meat. I found Rachel once, not all of her, but recognizable parts in the refrigerator. I'm sure she has stumbled across me as well.

"I wish I could see them," I say.

—∞—

Every night I count the snakes. Every night the snakes change position.

—∞—

There is a dream I have frequently. Holding my wife June's hand, looking into a crib where Delilah, a fresh squirming baby, opens her big blue eyes. I have never felt prouder. Matthew cries in the background. June squeezes my hand. One of us will have to leave the beautiful eyes to see what he is wailing about.

I wish it was a dream.

—∞—

We've tried every imaginable way to get out of the house. Once I managed to slip out the front door, or *was let out*, only to reemerge in my closet. Today I am in the attic, a stuffy and thick-dusted room with one window facing the street. There are several old boxes and pieces of broken furniture that have been here forever.

The casement window is cracked and caked with grime. It is so filthy I can't see anything, but I know the fog is still there, always. It's quiet downstairs, too quiet, and at the same time a thumping crosses over the roof right above me. The thumping is terrifying because it's coming from *outside*, but it moves on, as if it was oblivious to whatever is beneath it.

With a screwdriver I pry the window. It gives after my hands become numb with the effort. I push the window open. The fog rushes in, then settles on and mixes with the dust creating a sparkling carpet for an instant. I don't waste any time.

I squeeze through the window and scramble onto a sloped roof, holding onto the mushy rotted frame with one hand.

The frame snaps, silently. I tumble off the roof. There is no time to scream.

Rachel bends down, stares me straight in the eye. "What are you doing under my bed?"

—∞—

Dad uses hammers against the doors and the windows. Wood splinters. Glass shatters. Blood spills from his arms and hands. But in a blink, all is as it was.

The first night. The first week. The first month. Maybe years. There is no radio, television, internet, no glimpse of the outside world. We scramble and huddle and scream. Odd dreams and images assail us. I remember bits and pieces of school, friends, work (somewhere sitting in a cubicle before a computer), all these things stop-action pictures of our lives out *there*, moving on, while we are imprisoned *here*.

—⁕—

Dinner. Mom makes spaghetti, and we sit around a little oak table in the kitchen. I don't know where the table came from—it's not the one I remember Mom and Dad buying at the furniture store, but no one says anything about it, so I don't either. Rachel refuses to touch her spaghetti, says it squirms like a nest of worms. Dad ignores her but doesn't touch his either. He stares at the plate.

Normally we are chatterboxes at the table, but this time no one seems willing to talk. Like we are all holding secrets.

Mom breaks the quiet, speaking to Dad. "Do we know anything about the people that used to live here?" The question sounds oddly familiar.

Dad twirls a small bit of spaghetti on his fork, then scrapes it off on his plate. All the while staring through Mom like she isn't there. Dad is a tall man with broad shoulders and long arms, fit but with a slight paunch. His black hair is thinning. He generally wears a crooked smile like he knows something you don't. Tonight, he isn't smiling.

"An old couple, I think, lived here for thirty years or so. I don't know what happened to them." He looks down at his plate. "Or the people before them. This place is over a hundred years old."

"We're in our new house," Rachel says, eager to correct Dad. Everyone turns to her, and she looks back and forth to each of us, wondering if she said something wrong. For an instant she is a teenager with dyed red hair and multiple face piercings, scarecrow thin, hostile eyes darting everywhere. Then, in a flash, the six-year-old Rachel is back, a slight quiet moppet, the kind of kid that blends into any scene like a chameleon.

Mom smiles. Dad studies the table, then Rachel, and says, "Guess, I forgot." He laughs, a forced fake laugh, and we all laugh.

Then Rachel says, "But I've seen the people who used to live in the old house. They live here now."

Mom puts her smile back on, a shaky one that threatens to fall apart. "Honey, I'm sure you're imagining things."

Dad shifts uneasily in his seat. "What do they look like, Rachel?"

"Don't encourage her," Mom says through clenched teeth.

Rachel is beside herself. She wanted the attention, now she is sorry for being in the center of it. "They are so white, like Mom's china dolls. And they have old eyes, like how grandpa and grandma's eyes used to be. They watch me when I wake up in the morning."

"Stop it," Mom says.

"Go on," Dad says.

"At first, I was scared. Their arms sometimes go up and down like they're scratching at me or playing like they're cats. But they don't get close. I don't think they can get to me. I'm used to them now. And I don't think they want to hurt me. I think they just want out."

"Enough of this!" Mom jumps from the table. She glares at Dad, fists clenched, shaking. "No more of this nonsense. There's no one in her room!"

Mom flops out of the room like she had too much to drink. Dad doesn't say a word. When I look at my spaghetti it does look like worms swimming in blood.

—∞—

I wake up and see the ceiling, all wrong, and the walls, covered with wallpaper, spirals and strange geometric shapes. A lamp by the bed on a night table I don't recognize. And the bed itself is not the one I lay in last night when I went to bed. Did Mom or Dad somehow carry me to a different room while I was asleep? I throw off the quilt. *Where did that come from?*

It's a strange and unfamiliar room. When I go into the hall it's obvious that this isn't the house we moved into. I recognize features from the old house, the one that we watched being torn down, except everything is fresh, as if we had been transported back in time when the house was newly built and well taken care of. The wallpaper isn't ripped and hanging in threads, the wood floors are not water damaged and stained, and the place doesn't reek of mildew.

It is early morning. The hallway is dark but there is enough light filtering in from downstairs that I can see many closed doors and the stairs. I know there are four bedrooms, a closet, and a door that leads to the attic. I explored the place many times, only now the place is fixed up clean, and I wonder if I am still asleep, dreaming each step I take.

I go downstairs, moving agonizingly slow. Trembling. No sounds come from the kitchen. Someone should be up. I know I am in a dream. Something is shadowing me, I can feel it. Something just at the corner of my eye, a blurred movement, a disruption of light and space.

Whatever it is mimics my moves. And each time I whip around to look, it whips around at the same time so that the image, the feeling, is always out of reach at the edge of my vision.

The feeling of being watched and having something close to me that doesn't belong is overwhelming. I hustle into the kitchen, expecting it to be empty, but it's not. Mom and Dad are at the table. Glasses and utensils are all over the room, on the table, the counter, on top of the refrigerator and stove, even the chairs. It's as if they had a party during the night and never bothered to clean up. There's no food. Anywhere. The glasses are empty and dry.

Mom notices me in the doorway. She gives a little wave with her fingers, along with a vague smile. Dad's fingers are in his mouth. He's chewing, fresh lines of blood streaking down his chin, dripping onto the table.

—∾—

We keep to our rooms, Rachel and me. Dad screaming. Mom screaming. Things crash downstairs. A lot of thumping and screeching as if all the furniture is being moved and tossed about. After a long silence there is a knock at my door. The door opens a crack.

Dad says, "We can't get out."

—∾—

I think early on we all knew something dreadful had happened. We razed an old house to make room for a new one, a modern townhouse-style home with four bedrooms, three baths, open space design, a massive kitchen and living area, and a rooftop deck with a view of the mountains. I can't remember anything about that place except the stickers on the new windows.

We are now in the original old Tudor style house with casement windows, a small functional kitchen, three modest bedrooms, and a living room with a sooty, neglected fireplace. It had never been torn down. It was, and is, and always will be.

And the new house? I believe it's here too, only out of reach. Perhaps inhabited by the parts of us not drawn into this world. That explains the mysterious memories that slip into my head. We are trapped here, in these bodies, in a house that shouldn't exist, while we are at the same time moving on with our lives. *Out there.*

Rachel asked once, only once, if we were dead. Like the people she sees. I don't think so. I don't think the dead can feel pain. And we can feel. I can't explain how we come back after dying in gruesome ways. Rachel and I have talked about that, but we just don't know. Mom and Dad are too far gone—there is nothing human left behind their eyes. They die and come back repeatedly, but the house has taken something from them that it hasn't yet taken from Rachel and me.

There is no food in the pantry, hasn't been for a long time. We are ravenously hungry and have devoured every edible thing in the house until there is nothing left but each other. I don't know if the distant memories of killing each other for food are real or not. I don't want to know.

It doesn't matter. We come back anyway.

—⟋⟍—

Rachel disappears for long periods of time. I don't know where she goes, and she won't talk about it. She is always empty when I see her after these disappearances, and it is only after a long while that she becomes herself again. I suspect she has a place, like my closet, where she falls into a black abyss.

Mom and Dad pop out of nowhere. Sometimes they seem normal. Sometimes they are monsters beneath the familiar skin. We avoid them whenever possible.

I can't avoid the images that are fed into my brain, though. They are waking dreams. I am sure what I see and remember is real. Dad murdering Mom in the kitchen with a large butcher knife. Dad hacking at Mom with a hatchet. Hitting her with his fists. Mom catching Dad from behind with a baseball bat, the swing connecting so well and so hard his skull caves and splatters like a rotten pumpkin. Mom slicing Dad's throat like she is carving the leg from a turkey.

Blood is everywhere in these memory dreams. The killer, whether it is Dad or Mom, then turns their attention to Rachel and me. We run up the stairs to our rooms. The killer jiggles the door knobs but can't get in. They can never get in.

There have been a few times when we were caught. I can't think about that. It has become something of a game with Rachel and me, to see how close we can come to the murder action, to scamper to our safe rooms and shut the door at the last second. The killer pounds our doors and screams in frustration. Rachel giggles hysterically in her room each time.

I do the same.

—⟋⟍—

Delilah climbs an old ash tree in the backyard. She is fluid, moves like a spider, a natural athlete.

Matthew is downstairs playing video games. Every now and then I hear him laugh or shout. They are so young. And at this moment I feel so old.

June comes into the bedroom and stands next to me, watching our girl hang like a monkey from a branch about ten feet off the ground. We are not concerned. Delilah is safest when she's in the tree.

June puts her arms around me, and I know she is smiling, seeing our little girl out there so happy and free. I think of Mom and Rachel, long gone, how they would have enjoyed this moment, too.

"We should take pictures," June says. "Show them to your dad the next time we visit."

"Yeah," I say. "As if he would recognize us anymore."

I turn and see her beautiful face, tiny worry lines sprouting from the corners of her eyes.

I force a smile and give her a sideways hug. "Everything is going to be all right."

I let her go and turn back to the window. Delilah is gone. So is the ash tree. The few trees remaining in the window view are leafless and gnarled black against a gray sky. Everything is wrong. I gasp and spin, and June is gone, too.

—⁓—

Scratching outside my door. I am still disoriented from the waking dream, but I go to the door and slowly, cautiously, open it to see what's making the noise in the hallway.

Dad is opposite the bathroom, not far from the stairs. He is groaning, as if in pain, and his hands are raised above his head while he presses against the wall and moves along. His hips thrust in and out. He is licking the wall.

—⁓—

The holes grow bigger outside. Rachel joins me at the window. I feel the heat from her body and listen to her shallow breaths, but I don't look at her.

I once found Rachel hanging in her closet. She used a rolled-up sheet and tied it to the wooden rod, then tied the loose end about her neck while standing on a metal folding chair. She must have kicked the chair out from under her. She was apparently hanging there for some time. Her face swollen blue, the neck bent, swinging softly as if there was a breeze in the closet. I didn't scream or shout, simply held her limp body while I unwound the sheet and let her drop to the floor.

When she did, her eyes opened, and she gurgled for air.

Now Rachel shuffles when she walks, as if she's carrying a great load on her back. Her voice is so hoarse it's almost impossible to understand a word she says. The words are bent.

I don't like to see her this way. I wonder what she sees when she looks at me.

—⁓—

The fog is almost entirely gone now. Rachel presses her face against the window.

"Lorck," she slurs, pointing at something. There are people outside, in the yard. The sky is clear and blue, a light breeze disturbing the leaves of the trees across the street. A bulldozer is idling in the grass and dirt. Rachel giggles. I am tempted to run downstairs, get Mom and Dad, whatever their condition may be, show them what's happening *out there*. But I don't. If I take my eyes off what's happening outside, it might disappear.

Construction workers walk here and there. A family is gathered by the street watching the activity. The mother and father are hard to make out, but they seem young and familiar. A young boy, in shorts and T-shirt, about my age, with tousled blonde hair, watches the house. A little girl is sitting cross legged in the grass, preoccupied with dandelions.

Rachel squeals. The bulldozer starts toward the house. Everyone is watching the bulldozer but the boy. He stands straight and his eyes catch mine. I raise my hand.

He screams.

This is something of an experimental piece. I wanted to write a different type of haunted house story, one that shifted around in time and place with the intent of keeping the reader as disoriented as the characters. The idea of a house continuing to be haunted even after it had been torn down appealed to me, as well as the idea of parallel universes overlapping in certain places. Obviously inspired by House of Leaves *by Mark Z. Danielewski and some of Harlan Ellison's stuff (most notably "I Have No Mouth and I Must Scream").*

Once I had the image of a family watching the old place being scraped, I knew the story would come full circle and end with the family on the inside watching themselves on the outside. No happy ending.

A Light Just Out Of Range

Originally published in Deadman's Tome's March to the Grave, *2017*

The Western Front near the river Somme, November 1916

"You see that?" Delroy squinted and tried to make out the light he saw two hundred yards out in No Man's Land. It wasn't there now, as Finch turned his bulbous head to peer over the trench to the growing darkness ahead. Heavy drops of rain plopped into the mud and splattered into his face as he tried to get a look.

"Fuck no." Finch kept his head low. If the bloke next to him wanted his head blown off by a sniper, well, so be it. There was nothing out there to see anyway except mud, water filled shell holes, and belts of barbed wire. And, of course, the bloated stinking bodies from the previous day's action.

"I swear I saw it. Moving out thataway." Delroy leaned farther out than he should have to point. Finch reached over and grabbed his coat, pulling him down.

"You fuckin' crazy? You want to join Bax and Bloodlips out there in that stinkin' mess? God, man, get a grip."

"I saw a fucking light out there, moving around."

"This time, when night is drawing down you can see shit." Finch looked up at the dark sky, drops of rain pelting his face.

"It wasn't a star, if that's what you're saying. What if they're creeping up on us?"

"You gone daft? They ain't gonna announce themselves to us with lanterns. Here I am, shoot my ass." Delroy held his rifle tight. His hands numb.

His ears ringing from the shelling last night. Skin crawling with lice. And now he's seeing shit.

Sure. Finch was right. No one would walk around with a lantern, risk getting killed like that. He knew both armies sent out spies to lay in the shell holes or among the dead to watch what was going on with the other side. He knew sometimes truces were called to collect the dead. He knew what flares looked like. What artillery bursts were like. And he was fucking seeing things.

Delroy had seen too much action the past few weeks. By all rights he should be dead, like most of his friends. Now there was only a handful of soldiers left from the original company. Finch. Harmon. Jessups. Delroy was twenty-two going on sixty. All he thought about was cold rations, a bullet coming toward his eye, and the thousands of nightmare rats that haunted the trenches during the night.

Finch rested, back to the mud wall. The rain fell harder than before. They were standing on planks that barely offered any protection from rising water. Harmon and a new kid stood in shadows eight yards down near the officer's cave. It used to be Captain Mackelvie's quarters, but he was out there rotting away in the mud now, and a new officer and aide came on today. Delroy was sure all the officers wanted him dead, in fact he was convinced this silly war was concocted just to kill him. Delroy crept back up and peered over the parapet.

He saw a light. It moved, bobbled in the distance. It indeed did look like someone was carrying a lantern. He thought about firing toward the light, see what might happen. The way it went here and there, purposeful, methodical, it couldn't be a flare dropped by a parachute. It had to be somebody. "There it is, again," he said to Finch.

It was totally dark now, so Finch groaned and mumbled a barrage of curses when he raised his head to look. A light. It looked to be coming right at them. Far enough away that he thought it had to be as large as a lantern. Certainly not a cigarette. Not a flare. "Damn," he said.

What happened next surprised both men. The light rose upwards higher than any man could lift it. Finch aimed his rifle at the light and fired. The crack startled everyone around them in the trench, and there was a quick flurry of activity, bodies rushing against the wall, rifle barrels pointed up like barren corn stalks. It was so dark everyone splashed in the water and mud and bumped into each other. Loud curses erupted in this stench swell of body odor, vomit, and wet decay.

The new officer stumbled from his cave. "What the fuck," he said.

Someone pointed to Finch, and he splashed over, nearly losing his balance several times. "What is it?" he asked.

Finch strained to see where the light went, then satisfied it was gone, turned to the green captain. "Enemy patrol, I think, sir." He spoke evenly and held the captain's aggravated stare. "Delroy here saw a light bouncing around out there. I saw it, too. Took the fucker out." he paused. "Sir."

"What if it was one of our men?"

Finch shrugged. "Our men aren't so fucking stupid, sir."

The captain hoisted himself over the parapet and looked. The rain had settled a bit, but there was no moon, no stars, but black punctuated by brief lightning blasts of artillery deep in the distance. Satisfied there was nothing there, the captain made a harumph and scuttled back down into the trench. Looking at both Delroy and Finch, he said, "If you see it again, the light, I want you to let me know. Likely it's the enemy picking at their dead, or ours."

"There it is!" Harmon, a grizzled veteran of this never-ending battle, stood on the fire step, using his rifle and bayonet to point. The men at once peered over the parapet and saw a light in the distance, dancing, it seemed, over the countless corpses and craters of No Man's Land.

"Jesus," the captain said. "Thought you got the bugger."

Finch was astounded. He looked to Delroy, who took aim and, without waiting for an order, fired at the light. This time the light didn't go out. It was motionless for several long seconds, then swung gently like a pendulum. "It's got to be closer to us than them," he said.

Harmon said, "Looks like someone waving us to come on." He turned to the captain. "Got to be one of ours. They didn't fire back."

The captain, new to the front, uniform still relatively fresh and free of piss and shit stench, stood quiet and reflective.

Finch said, "It's likely a trap to draw some of our boys out, then mow 'em down." He got close to the captain to make his point. "It's a dark rainy night, and No Man's Land is the worst place on the planet. Besides, it's been quiet tonight. Very little artillery fire and rifle reports to break the mood. Why take any risks?"

The captain shook his head. "You, you, you." He pointed to Delroy, Finch, Harmon, then to a new kid who was shivering so hard out of fear and cold Delroy thought he would break apart. A group of soldier shadows that had been approaching to see what the fuss was about suddenly turned and disappeared into the convoluted trench blackness as soon as they heard the captain choosing volunteers. "You men sneak up on that light and see what the fuck is going on out there. See if it's one of ours, maybe someone wounded. Don't engage if it's the enemy unless you're found out. Report back in two hours." Sergeant Major Rawlings joined the captain out of nowhere, as if magically summoned to enforce the captain's command.

"That's crazy," stammered Finch. "It's just as likely a German patrol as one of ours. Anyone who goes out into No Man's Land don't come back."

The sergeant major cleared his throat. "We send out patrols all the time and they almost always come back. You've been on some of them yourself, Finch. Now, you've been given an order, men. You got five minutes to get your gear and get going. Two shots when you're coming back in." Rawlings and the captain spun away and were gone.

"Damn you, Delroy, and your damned lights." Finch slapped his soaked trousers. "Boys, we got a date with the devils."

"What do you mean?" the new recruit asked.

"Finch here thinks there's ghouls out there, live underground in tunnels and such. Don't you, Finch?" Delroy slung his rucksack over his shoulder, pulled a hook knife out of its sheath, looked it over, put it back in.

"I didn't want to say it before, but I've heard things about what's out there," Finch said, checking his rifle. He faced the shivering lad, sure that the boy's face was as green as the pus that spills out a gangrenous arm. "I've heard they was real ghouls, monsters that live deep underground." He turned and gestured toward the blackness that was No Man's Land. "They come out at night and feast on the dead bodies. I heard they prefer live ones."

Finch stood on the fire step, rifle and bayonet slung over his back. "I also heard other stories about men who live under the ground out there— deserters mostly, don't matter what country, they're all banded together— come out at night to strip the dead, take their weapons, maybe take body parts to eat, I don't know. You been here a while, you hear stories." A twisted smile when he looked the kid in the eyes.

"He's fucking with you," Harmon said, slapping the kid on the back. "Fairy tales, is all." The kid looked more scared than ever. "Don't lose your head out there, or you'll get us all killed. First time belly down on the mud, lad, pretend you're a bloody snake."

The four men blackened their faces with shoe polish and made sure they were well equipped for a reconnaissance mission: knives, hatchets, revolvers, trench shovel, wire cutters, compass. When ready they silently tumbled over the parapet and started moving toward the light in the distance, still there, still seeming to beckon them. The silence the men moved into was of the dead. It was pitch black except for the distant light that played before them and occasional flashes from way-distant artillery.

"It looks further away than ever," Delroy whispered to Finch.

When they reached the wire entanglement zone they had to crawl in a zigzag line through known breaks in the wire. Several German soldiers were splayed on the wire in stiff death poses. Delroy brushed past one poor fellow who was curled in a fetal position, as if tossed into the barbed wire by some maniacal giant. The part he brushed against came with him as he crawled on, the death stench and juices now a part of his own clothing. A spittle of vomit rose in his throat. Finch was about two yards to his right. The others were shortly behind, making their own way through the sucking mud. The light was clear. He wondered, *Why hadn't the Germans reacted to it?*

He whispered to Finch to stop. "It looks like a lantern," he said, as quietly as possible. They were still a good distance from the German trenches, and now clear of their own side's barbed wire entanglements. He knew flares could be sent up any moment if the Germans suspected their whereabouts, and he dreaded being caught out in the open when their machine guns opened up. They were out of earshot, he was sure of that, but he wondered if the Germans had patrols of their own crawling about.

Finch mumbled a succession of curses. "I figure we're in the middle of Hell. That's the devil for sure waving us on." He lined the light up in his sights. "I can pick that damn light off at this distance. Don't know about what's holding it, though."

"You'll draw every machine gun, too. We're in range." The smell of hundreds of bodies decaying in the mud and water-filled shell holes supported his claim.

Harmon and the fresh kid slurped up to them, more swimming in the muck than crawling. They studied the light. They all saw something different. Harmon thought it looked like a star, so bright in the pitch dark it gave off a halo. Delroy was convinced it was a lantern, held by someone, likely a wounded soldier. Finch thought it was something demonic, that somehow one of the craters that pockmarked the battlefield opened into the jaws of Hell. The fresh kid saw a faint dot of light that blinked, like an errant ember from a fire drifting on the wind.

"We got to get closer," Delroy said. "We see what the fuck it is, then we git the hell back." Two days before they were about this far into No Man's Land, making a great push to overwhelm the Germans. They didn't get any further. He saw his friend Corporal Bloodlips blown into a dozen pieces. Second Lieutenant Hastings lost his face right next to him. It was a slaughter. A few men made it to the German barbed wire, which were supposed to have been blown to smithereens by the artillery bombardment, but the wire was still there. Those soldiers became gory red-green ornaments on the hedgerows of wire.

The four men moved forward on elbows and knees, heading toward the light. They could make out the silhouettes of blackened tree stalks from its glow. They avoided the shell holes when they could, although several times one of them would slip down and roll about in the water and mud, made putrescent by decaying bodies. The fresh kid lost his rifle when he fell in one hole; Finch pulled him out and clamped his hand over the kid's mouth to keep him from screaming. Frogs croaked about them as they slithered back to Delroy and Harmon.

Now they heard shots, coming from the German trenches.

"They're firing at the light, too," Harmon said. "I think I can make out someone by the light."

"There," Delroy said. He did see someone, or something, waving what appeared to be a lantern. They were about forty yards from the shadowy figure. The light was blinding at this distance. Delroy thought about the legends of the ghouls and the bands of deserters who lived deep beneath this hell. He had heard the stories too, as well as Finch. But no one could survive in No Man's Land, no matter how deep their tunnels. Delroy felt himself sinking in the mud and slime—if you stopped crawling for any length of time that's what'll happen. He edged closer to the others. The kid was whimpering, out of his head. It was all Finch could do to hold him down, keep him from running off.

"The light is coming at us," Harmon said. The light seemed to swivel about, at the same time rising and falling, as if someone was trying to move toward them in the uneven, muddy terrain.

"Whoever or whatever it is can't know we're here. You can't see five yards in front of your face. But if that light…" He struggled with the kid. "Stop it. You'll get us all killed."

Finch slapped him then, the boy falling backwards into the muck. A nearby rat squealed sharply and moved from the body it had been feeding on. Delroy and Finch watched the silhouette of the bloated thing, easily the size of a large cat, take its time sauntering toward the light. "Jesus," Finch said.

The figure with the light stopped twenty yards out. It looked like a man, but they couldn't discern what the light was—it was not a flare or a torch and seemed to be too round to be a lantern. Sometimes the light swelled, and other times diminished, as if it were a living, breathing thing, an extension perhaps of the man or demon holding it. The man brought his arm up, holding the bulb of light to his face.

Finch slammed his fist into his own mouth, biting his tongue in the process. He fell back with a short scream, thrashing his arms in the sludge. His hand slid into a body like it was rancid butter, the same body the rat had been feasting on. All this as his brain shattered in recognizing the man holding the light, Corporal Bloodlips. As Finch sank near the putrid body, he felt something tugging his leg. Pulling him down. Before he could scream again the mud poured into his throat like an avalanche.

Delroy scrambled forward, then stopped as he remembered seeing Bloodlips blown apart. *This is not happening*, he thought. *It can't be Bloodlips.*

At that moment Harmon was up, taking ungainly steps trying to run toward the thing before them, the mud sucking him down to the knees. "He's one of ours," he cried.

Delroy screamed, "Don't!" Just as machine gun fire erupted from the German line. Harmon spun like a marionette and fell as the thing with the light advanced. He was swallowed by the mud. Delroy buried himself as bullets popped by. When the firing stopped, he looked for Finch and the kid. The kid was still there, only a few feet away, convulsing with fear but untouched as far as he could tell.

He crawled to the kid, shook him, and said, "We got to get back, hear?"

The kid nodded.

Bloodlips was almost on them, moving through the devastated terrain like he was walking on water. It *was* Bloodlips. Behind Bloodlips were others. Ten, fifteen figures falling out of the shadows, shambling toward the two frozen soldiers. Somehow Delroy knew Mackelvie, Hastings, and all his comrades lost in the battle over the past few weeks were there, coming for him.

Delroy took aim and fired at the thing masquerading as Bloodlips. The light he had been holding was now gone. The entire figure of Bloodlips was aglow instead. His bullet went nowhere or simply disappeared into the emanation. Bloodlips was almost upon them.

He pulled the kid to his knees and they scrambled backwards, falling and thrusting their bodies away from the approaching menace. Delroy's rifle dropped and disappeared in the darkness. How far to their own lines? It didn't matter. They had to keep moving. Thoughts disintegrated. It was animal survival.

They crawled for what seemed hours. Intermittent shots punctured the air. Several times each man got caught in wire and had to be pulled loose by the other. Delroy's legs felt like they were totally shredded, but he couldn't stop. When he finally glanced back to see where Bloodlips was, there was nothing. Whatever they had seen before was gone.

The kid now urged him on. "Keep moving," he said. "I saw Finch sucked down. It was so quick I couldn't do nothing about it. Those things must've gotten him. They're under us."

The blind fear that had propelled them this far was dissipating. Delroy thinking, *Don't want our own men shooting at us when we come up on them.*

Thinking, *What do I tell the captain about Finch and Harmon?*

Thinking, *No one will believe what we saw out there.*

Thinking, *Bloodlips, Hastings, all the others dead, wanting us to join them. Now Finch and Harmon are among them. A ghost army...*

Suddenly Delroy was stopped. Stuck on something beside a shell hole. He heard squeaks as the kid crawled ahead of him. He had little feeling left in his legs and arms, but a stabbing pain brought it all back with a blinding paralysis. Something was tearing at him, no, biting his legs. A rat's head burst from the mud inches from his face. Delroy screamed.

It was a scream that turned the heads of thousands of men scattered in trenches on both sides of the Western Front. It was a scream that hung in the air and settled on the skin like acid, burning its way to the core of whatever consciousness remained in the hollow-eyed soldiers left in the trenches to continue the war.

The kid scurried through the mud. He didn't look back. He didn't see the dozens of giant rats twisting and turning Delroy's body in a feeding frenzy. Fresh blood.

The kid was found in the morning, hung on the wire in the entanglements. A brave volunteer moved out during Stand To—the time at dawn when the entire British line is on guard for an attack—and cut him free. There was no sniper activity, and he was brought safely in. The captain asked him his name and what became of the others. The kid said nothing. There was nothing inside. He was hollowed out.

Veteran soldiers knew what they were seeing. The kid had shell shock. They took him away on a stretcher, curled in a fetal position. The soldiers went back to their mundane, boring routine of life in the trenches.

Shortly after dusk a soldier reported to the new captain that there were sightings of a light moving about, well into No Man's Land.

"A Light Just Out of Range" was written for an anthology call concerning the horrors of war. I wanted to write something about World War I, and while

doing research about the Battle of the Somme and No Man's Land, I came across legends about the "wild men" of No Man's Land. These were popular legends during the conflict. Some stories depicted wild men, deserters most likely, who inhabited No Man's Land, hiding in tunnels during the day and coming out at night to forage for food and supplies. Other stories depicted ghouls who feasted on the bodies of freshly killed soldiers. There is no basis of truth in any of the legends, but they were enough to spark some ideas for my own story.

My 1963 Ford Galaxie
And The Maniacs
Of Dearborn County

Originally published in Deadman's Tome, 2016

A turbulent blue sky washed across the man's open dead eyes before I shut the trunk over his ugly-assed face. This was the third one today, and there was plenty of room in the oversized trunk to accommodate many more guests. Once, a hundred years ago, I smuggled eight friends and acquaintances into the Twin Drive-In, and there was still room for beer and rotgut wine in the trunk. The car is a beast.

I checked on Katie. She was frozen in the front seat, her mouth still open after that long piercing scream that brought me running from the lake where I was filling a bucket of water for the radiator. Lucky she was in the car and could roll up the window before the maniac got to her. He was still scratching and kicking at the passenger side door when I caught him from behind with my tire jack, which fortunately I had carried with me to the lake for protection. I ran out of bullets the day before, thanks to the maniac's trunk companions.

"It's okay." I tossed the tire jack in the backseat. Then, realizing there was blood on it, I reached over and wiped it with a greasy towel that covered the little basket of food and beer we had scavenged from an abandoned house a few miles back.

"We should have stayed there," she said in a quivering voice.

I moved around and opened the driver's side door, took a good clean look around us to make sure we were truly alone, then pulled myself in the car like one of those astronauts squeezing into a Mercury capsule. "No," I said, "not a good idea. We got to keep moving. We got gas, we got hope."

She looked at me like I was crazy, her face twisted and scrunched. I could see she was running through all the crazy shit that had happened to us the past two days. I could see, too, that she was stuck. She wanted to stay put somewhere, hole up and wait this thing out. I was determined to ride out from trouble with my tank of a car. "What if…"

I cut her off. "Don't go there," I said. "We get out of this county, out of this country, we'll be all right. I just know it."

"You left me alone."

"The car was locked. I didn't want to wake you up." Now she was letting it settle in. Puffs of blonde hair fell to her forehead. Streams of tears fell, too, as she really shook this time. I thought she was beautiful, and I wanted to do it right then and there, in the front seat, but she was so scared, so…helpless. "The car was overheating. There was steam coming out and everything, so I stopped to get a little water. No way I would've left you here alone if I thought one of those maniacs was nearby." I brushed her face with my fingers. She didn't pull back. Good. I scooted closer. How long have I owned this car? Six months? And I never had the opportunity to make love to a pretty girl in the front seat. Until now.

I cupped her breast. She slapped me so hard my head bounced off the leather seat like a basketball hitting the metal rim of the hoop.

"Shit." I rubbed my cheek.

"You left the window down, you stupid shit. That maniac could've gotten me, and all you're thinking about is getting laid. Fuck you." She crossed her arms.

I stared at her for several minutes, noting the crust of blood and grease on her arms and legs, delicate blonde hairs poking through in spots, a rebirth of life in the ash after a volcanic explosion. "I'll get the water," I said. "Keep the windows up."

Twenty minutes or twenty years later we were on the road again, zigzagging past empty rusted cars and carcasses of dead farm animals placed strategically in our way like some sick obstacle course. Katie didn't say a word, just stared ahead and took deep breaths every time I swerved or ran over something.

Katie was all I had. I was convinced, somehow, she'd loosened the radiator hose, fucked up my car so we would have to stop, make a stand, stop running. How else did she get grease on her fine arms and legs? If we stopped someplace, I was going to sleep where I could keep an eye on the car. My Ford Galaxie was everything. I loved that car.

I swear I didn't know Katie before this, didn't know she existed. I found her just outside what was left of Carlsville, standing by the side of the road like a mileage sign. I should have assumed she was a maniac like everyone else, but I didn't. She didn't look crazy. I stopped. She had to have given up, to be standing there out in the open, waiting for who knows what.

The way I saw it, she must've been waiting for *me*. Maniacs don't drive cars. She got in the car before I said a word and we high tailed it out of there, my 1963 Ford Galaxie blazing a slippery trail through the wilderness of bloody guts and farm machinery, car hulks and skin-shredded splinters of horse and cow legs, and the occasional dead maniac on or off the road. The smell of death numbing and reassuring after we gave in and rolled the windows down from the stifling heat.

We've been together a long time now. Two or three days maybe. Time being pretty screwed up.

I can't remember when it happened, the Change, although I'm sure it wasn't too long ago. It seemed like I only had my car, my first, a few months. And although everything is a little hazy, there are some memories of driving to and from high school, my buddies Chad, Nolan, and Bill kicking it up, partying like there was no tomorrow. Kidding me about my Mayberry car. I have no memory before the Ford Galaxie. I suppose it's the trauma. Snapshots of my parents as we looked over the car before buying it. A 1963 Ford Galaxie 500XL 260 V8 Cruise-A-Matic, three years old and the only one like it in the entire county. My dad saying nothing bad could ever happen to me with *that car.*

Then the Change. I woke up in the backseat of my car after a hard night partying, and it had already happened. I slept right through it.

Dead bodies everywhere. Most of the buildings crumbled shells, including my house and my high school. Everyone I knew and cared about was gone, and in their place were unrecognizable rotting bodies. And maniacs who come out of nowhere like surprise jack-in-the-boxes who try to hurt and eat you.

I have five maniac bodies in my spacious trunk. Chad and Bill were the first occupants. They were gnawing on each other in front of the main library, or the rubble that had been the main library. I drove up on them, then over them when they came at me with mouths agape, grunting and wheezing like they had each swallowed a longneck bottle of Strohs. I cried like a baby, then lifted their crumpled bodies into the trunk. Don't know why I'm keeping them in the trunk. Guess it makes me feel safer, knowing where they are and all. They can't come back when they're locked in there, although someday one of them could spring out like a jack-in-the…

I drove out of town. I drove and drove through the valley of the shadow of, well, you know, the point being that things were really screwed up. There were occasional gas stations that somehow escaped the carnage, and I was able to fill up, add oil and water and all that stuff. I missed the full service. I missed the parade of cars cruising through the main street of Aurora, engines revving, the smell of exhaust and fried food. The music loud, each passing wave of lyrics. Tell me over and over and over again, my friend, we're on the eve of "sugar pie honey bunch," you know "papa's got a brand-new bag," "don't let on, don't say she's broke my heart…"

There are cars scattered everywhere, but their radios are silent now. I think I drove about a thousand miles before I stumbled on Katie.

She didn't say a word at first. Just stared at me and the car, a look of disbelief that we were actually *moving*. Then she spoke. "I know you." I must have looked puzzled because she followed that with, "The Frisch's Drive-in. Carlsville?"

My eyes stayed fixed on dodging all the debris in the road. Still, I managed to shake my head. *You're cute, kinda, but I don't remember…*

"I was a carhop. I remember you, your friends, this car."

"Yeah, maybe. I guess we did hit the Carlsville Frisch's a few times."

"I remember this car because one of your asshole friends hit me with an empty beer can, hit the tray I was carrying, spilling shit all over the place. You tore outta there like a bat outta hell."

"Sorry. I think that was Bill who threw it. He's in the trunk, if you want to say something to him."

She was quiet for a minute. "This car doesn't go very fast," she said. "At least it's roomy."

She tried the radio now. Nothing. Static. She cried in a subdued innocent way, the way a fox might after stumbling into a trap and exhausting itself trying to find a way through the steel jaws. We drove on and on. I had never been out of Dearborn County before. I was eager to see the rest of the world.

—⚶—

It seems so long ago, but like I said, time is so screwed up. I thought Katie was sleeping again, but she must've been thinking about the maniac who almost got her.

"I think he was just trying to get in the car," she said.

"What do you mean?"

"I think he was scared."

"You were the one scared. He was a maniac. He wanted you for lunch."

The road bumped on, and I was all over it, the engine grinding and struggling to haul the metal beast strapped to it.

I felt her eyes on me the whole time, waiting, then she said, "I think they're like us. Only they're more scared than we are. They have nowhere to go."

"You're thinking too much," I said.

"Those two we killed this morning, I bet they only wanted in the house. This guy wanted in the car. I don't think he wanted me."

"Well, he's in the car now."

—⁂—

Katie wasn't really all that helpless. She was stirred up enough to help kill those two maniacs who stormed the house that morning. Or was it last month? I didn't remember how I came to have a hand cannon that took off one of the maniac's hands, nor what happened to that same gun after we drove away. I had this fleeting image of Katie swinging a baseball bat at the head of the other one and connecting with a home run. I didn't know what happened to the bat.

Didn't know where the food came from, but it was there in the basket in the backseat, suggesting we were on our way to a picnic. Andy and Helen and Barney and Thelma Lou, me and Katie.

Katie didn't talk about her family or her friends or anything at all really, the words that bubbled out elusive and distant, the way a hitchhiker would be careful about not sharing too much.

"We're still in Dearborn County," Katie said after a long bout of silence.

"I don't recognize anything," I said. "I know every inch of every road in Dearborn County, and we should be halfway across the country by now." I swerved to avoid an overturned tractor with a glistening arm bone jutting from underneath it. Bare leafless trees leaned over us on this stretch. We were so far out in nowhere.

"Should be a city or town somewhere," she mumbled. She drew her legs up under her and closed her eyes. Her trembling fingers not too far from my knee. I sped around a curve then another unexpectedly, the back wheels sliding just enough to jolt me into thinking we were going to melt into any number of lifeless trees. I braked hard and slid to a stop.

A maniac stood in the middle of the road. She was naked and dirty and wore a grin that reached around her face like Bozo the Clown. She was screaming at this marvelous white machine in front of her, screaming something about missiles, and mushrooms and the Russians, and the Red

Threat, and Lucy and Cuba, and clouds that shouldn't be, and she came at us. So fast I blinked, and she was on the hood of my car, my Ford Galaxie XL, scrambling toward the windshield on gnawed-to-the-bone fingers like some sort of crayfish skittering on a wet rock.

I screamed. Katie screamed. I stomped the gas pedal, throwing the maniac's flat squished face into the windshield. Then she, it, the maniac tumbled off. I sped away at top speed, looking in the rearview mirror to see if the thing was getting back up, then the car dropped over a rise and the image was replaced with empty road. I thought about going back, making sure it was dead, adding it to the trunk. But Katie was already freaked. There was no turning back.

We didn't talk. I knew what she was thinking. That maybe getting in the car with me was not a good idea. That maybe she was giving up. If I slowed down, she would toss herself out, end it once and for all. I didn't want to be alone. I couldn't slow down.

Stars streamed past the Galaxie as we neared light speed. Maniacs fell from the sky in blooming parachutes. The wipers scraped them off the windshield. Katie huddled against the door with her eyes closed. I heard her thoughts pounding away like a jackhammer. *Why are we still in Dearborn County after all this time? What if that lady wasn't a maniac, like you say? What if she was trying to tell us something?* Her thoughts ran on and on. *This car is ancient. It doesn't belong here. We don't belong here. That's why we have to stop.*

The world flipped a switch, and all that remained, all that mattered, was my 1963 Ford Galaxie 500 XL, still in pristine condition after three years and forty-odd thousand miles. Katie thought it was slow, but it was steady Eddie and true, true as could be, what the fuck did she know, anyway?

Dearborn County is as big as the United States of America. Hell, it spreads into and over the ocean like a baby's blanket, and some of these roads could be in France, or Germany, anywhere. The scenery doesn't matter. *Yes, Katie, we are still in Dearborn County. Yes, Katie, the maniacs are a figment of my 260-horse powered brain, there is nothing to be afraid of. Katie, you are lucky to be with me in this car. Nothing bad can ever happen to us in here.*

"No," she said. "We've got to stop. Find out if there are others. Give them a chance." She said she couldn't go on, not like this. Not with me.

I didn't say anything. We were the last two. I knew this. She should've been grateful for that. Should've been grateful to be with me. And every maniac we came up against was a painful reminder that the world had ended as we knew it. Katie needed to embrace the truth. But the maniac behind her closed eyelids could never do that.

"Isn't it obvious?" she said. "It will always be 1966 and we will always be stuck here in Dearborn County, and there will always be maniacs in your head chasing after you. I don't want to be a part of this any longer. I don't want to be driving around in this fucking piece of junk."

At some point I knew we would run out of road, or gas, or maniacs, and we would have only each other. Right. The hate that seeped from her eyes told me otherwise. There was no *us*, not in her mind, anyway. I didn't want to be alone. I didn't want to stop. I knew what I had to do. There was plenty of room in the trunk. I love this car.

The road straightened out. Before us an expanse of flat, untended farmland. A house in the distance, a blip on the horizon where the green sun was setting into swirling blue clouds, death's feather finally dropping onto the earth.

A 1963 Ford Galaxie 500 XL was my first car, and I loved that car. I think I bought it in 1970 and it truly was a tank of a car. You can squeeze a lot of teenagers in that car, and it was perfect for drive-in theaters, because two of us could sit in the front seats, and five or six kids could sneak in while hiding in the trunk.

Somehow, I came up with the idea of writing about that car. The title, "My 1963 Ford Galaxie and the Maniacs of Dearborn County," came to me first, and the story seemed to write itself after that. It was one of the few times where I literally felt like I was possessed by a friendly muse, and aside from some minor research about the time period, I wrote and completed the story in about two days' time. It was fun to write, even if nothing seems to make much sense. I like ambiguity.

That car has resurfaced a few times in other stories I've had published, and I imagine it will continue to do so. And Dearborn County is a real place in southwest Indiana, near Cincinnati, Ohio where I grew up.

Private Franks

Originally published in Shrieks and Shivers *from The Horror Zine, 2015.*

I stood up in my stirrups and gazed straight ahead, east toward the ridge at what appeared to be white rocks shining in the morning sun. "Boulders," I said.

"No." Godfrey said, almost dropping his field glasses. "Those are bodies."

I wiped my mouth, then pulled my hat brim closer to my eyes. My tongue felt along the dryness that crusted my lips. We rode our mounts slowly past the remains of several of our comrades as we ascended the ridge. Now more shapes, naked and bloated, were scattered along the ridge, leading to a cluster of bodies at the highest point within a half-circle of rotting horse carcasses.

The stench was terrific. We covered our mouths and noses as best we could with bandanas and ripped pieces of clothing. Several men bolted towards the river to vomit. A sickening buzz drowned out the wind rustling the high grass. Our Crow scouts, Half Yellow Face and Hairy Moccasin, turned back and rode off as fast as they could, as if they had seen hordes of ghosts.

Godfrey and I dismounted. Benteen rode further to the cluster of bodies and dismounted there.

"Jesus," I mumbled.

The body closest to me, if it could still be called that, was missing its head, hands, and feet. Something had fed on its abdomen leaving blotches of entrails trailing away into the grass. I bent over retching, but there was nothing in me to come up. Godfrey cried.

All the bodies were naked, except for an occasional sock on an unattached foot. Some of them were blackened from the sun or from the swarms of blue-green flies covering the wounds.

Someone mumbled, "Animals had at 'em. All of 'em." All that remained of a few of the soldiers just beyond where I stood were cracked and splintered bones with a few ribbons of tendon and flesh, the bones tossed about as if caught in a whirlwind of starving wolves and coyotes. There were no paw prints, although there was plenty evidence of moccasins and bare feet and boots and hoof prints, everywhere in the blood-dusty battleground.

We were silent. Some of the men sobbed and, as others rode up, they dismounted and joined us without a word, staying motionless for an eternity to take in the massacre around us. Benteen motioned for Godfrey and me.

The rest of the men stayed back as we walked toward him, leaving our horses with Private Jenks, who shook so hard we had to press the reins in his hands to make him understand what we wanted. Benteen pointed to his right. There, on the flat crest at the far end of the ridge lay Custer, naked. He was leaning in a half-sitting position against two slain troopers. He hadn't been torn apart like the others. A gunshot wound to the left temple. He had not been scalped.

"They're all gone," Benteen said. "They left him untouched. Don't know why." He kicked a spent cartridge out of his way and came over to me. He hadn't covered his face like the rest of us. He pulled a dusty and blood spotted bandana from his back pocket and did so now.

"Lieutenant Windolph. Have the men spread out. See if there are any…" His voice faded. I knew what he meant and nodded. He turned to Lieutenant Godfrey. "Take two men, go back and get shovels or whatever you can find." He kicked at the dust again, sending another cartridge into a dead horse.

Benteen walked a few yards from the General to another body, this one torn completely apart, as if some great beast had ravaged him instead of hostiles. His head was flattened. And again, it appeared he had been fed upon. On what remained of an arm nearby was a tattoo with the initials TWC. "That would be Tom," Benteen whispered. The General's brother.

The wind picked up. It rolled over the high grass and carried with it the stench of rotting flesh and sated flies. We spread out, being careful where we stepped, body parts everywhere. Scattering tufts of reddish-brown grass on the almost ashy white soil, a scene of loneliness and despair. Every man tired, thirsty, numb. For two days we had choked on dust and smoke with little water, withstanding one attack after another from the same bands that wiped out our commander.

The scouts were in awe of the Indians attacking us, saying that they had never before felt or seen such big medicine. When Terry and Gibbon's columns arrived, they found Custer and his men first, then found us hunkered down on a hill, expecting to die any moment. After a brief rest Benteen and a handful of us were ordered to this hellish place, to see for ourselves what happened to our comrades and friends.

The men were quiet. Heads down, searching, trying to find anyone we could recognize. My arm ached from a grazing I had received two nights back. I was lucky. Matthews was not. The bullet that skinned me hit him full in the forehead. I thought of him as I checked the corpses, hoping to find someone intact and not half eaten. Everything of any value was gone, taken away: weapons, ammunition, equipment, clothing. Occasionally a partial body with a bloody undershirt, or trousers, or socks was found, but any names stitched on the items was always cut out.

"Over here!" Pvt. Bennings on his knees, vomit erupting from his mouth as he tried to call out again. He was about thirty feet from the top of the ridge. I got to him first, seeing right away what he saw: a bloody fly-covered trouser leg protruding from the belly of a bloody sorrel. The leg moved.

"My God," I said. We both grabbed the leg and pulled, and the dead horse gave birth to a blubbering brown-red mess of a man. The man, covered in blood and rotting horse entrails, flailed at us and emitted a high-pitched bark, a dry attempt for a scream. "Take it easy, soldier," I said. "We're your friends."

Several other soldiers were there immediately and held the man down while we checked him for injuries. There was a festering wound on his right arm, a good chunk of flesh missing with what appeared to be tooth marks surrounding the wound. I did not recognize him in this condition, but Bennings said he thought it was Franks, a scrawny recruit from out east. He had avoided being slaughtered by somehow hiding inside the dead horse. For two days.

We poured water on his face while he was being held down. He took deep breaths and took the canteen with trembling hands and gulped the water down, threw it back up, then drank some more. This calmed him, but I could tell by his eyes he was quite mad. He looked at each of us, muttered something about the end of everything, being hungry, then closed his eyes.

I leaned over him. I heard one of the troopers say, "Damn coward."

I turned around and said, "What would you do?"

Before I could turn back Franks was on me, lurching up like an explosive charge, fixing his teeth on my arm at the very spot I had been wounded. I screamed and thrust my other arm against his head, hard, knocking him back, and out. Fresh blood oozed down my left arm. I stumbled backward into Godfrey and the others.

"Take him back to camp," I said, regaining my calm. Bennings and a few others threw him across a pony and rushed away through the grass toward the Bighorn River, then disappeared behind a bend. After more men from Gibbon's outfit arrived, we spent the rest of the day burying the remains of five companies in shallow graves and one large mass grave, using picks, axes, knives, cups, and raw blistered hands.

—∞—

"He wants to see you," Porter, the company surgeon, said. He had finished dressing my arm, leaned back and lit a thick cigar. "Franks' arm is gangrenous. It's going to have to come off."

"That's the least of his problems."

The doctor stared at me. "Oh, no, Charles. He's quite lucid now. He wants to see you, the man who helped pull him out of that horse." He smiled, displaying blackened teeth. "The man he took a bite out of."

"Franks spent two days inside a rotting horse. Everyone around him massacred, mutilated beyond recognition. How is it he survived, escaped detection?"

"Luck, I suppose. Go see him. Lt. Godfrey will go with you. He won't talk to anyone without you there. Let's see what he says happened down there."

Private Franks was tied to his cot. He looked barely human, pale, emaciated, his bad arm wrapped and oozing green pus, stinking up the tent. Half Yellow Face, one of the Crow scouts, and Corporal Lansing, interpreter, joined us. A number of men wanted to come along, curious to see the lone survivor of Custer's engagement, but the doctor thought it best to keep it to just a few men.

Franks was awake. His eyes were black shadows in the dim light inside the tent. The skin of his face dried and shrunken like old gauze. He wiggled against the ropes. Smiled as we came in.

"You remembered me?" I asked.

"Yes. I remember all of it."

"Well?" He kept his eyes on me, fixed, those black holes spearing into me as easily as the hundreds of arrows protruding from the dead we buried that day. "Tell us what happened."

"You won't believe me."

"Try us."

Franks took a deep breath and began his story.

I was with C Company. We rode into the river toward the village, but the General stopped. I guess he thought there were too many of you, changed his mind.

They were like bees knocked outta their hive, swarming up at us, shooting and picking us off as we sat dumb on our ponies waiting to move. Finally, the General hauled up toward the ridge. We scrambled after, holding up on a hill with Keogh and most of C Company, waiting for you to come…but you never came. They came at us, but we set them back, giving the General time to make it further up the ridge.

Then…they came at us again. So many. Stormed over our skirmish lines. A roar filled the air. Horses screaming, hooves pounding, Indians, soldiers yelling. You could even hear the sound of bones and skulls cracking, and over all this the deafening blasts of close-quarters rifles and pistols firing. I shot one bastard in the face. He was running so hard he didn't know he was dead, knocked me down. I tried to push him off, get back in the fight. Boots were kicking up dust and blood around me. I rolled over and out from the son of a bitch and knelt by James, who had crawled to me with an arrow in his eye. He still had fight in him. He stood and swung his useless jammed rifle about like a windmill, scaring the savages back like the devil he was.

Funny thing. The Indians pulled back. There were fewer shots. Keogh choked orders to regroup. Those of us who could move started backing up the hill toward where the rest of the Seventh was. I can still see the General, plain as day, standing up there with his brother trying to figure out what the Indians were up to, their horses already down and dead to give some protection, and maybe they thought it was over. Some troopers fired shots but there was nothing to aim for 'cept an occasional head popping up outta the grass. I knew there had to be thousands of them, and they had us good.

We were waiting for reinforcements. We thought for sure you would come. We were praying you would come.

I couldn't figure why they were waiting, why they didn't just come on, already. It got real quiet. Eerie quiet. A wind kicked up. A cold wind like blows on the plains in winter. Icy cold, lieutenant. It numbed our faces and worse, our fingers. My rifle dropped outta my hands like it was a wisp of smoke. Terror gripped me. It welled up from the inside, this feeling we were all going to die in some horrible way. I think we all thought that, because every one of us had that hopeless fear look that froze us to the bloody ground like statues. Those seconds lasted years.

Suddenly, screams outta the sky. A cloud of death blew across us, thick of decay and rancid meat, burning our nostrils and throats. And following that cloud, hundreds of warriors, giant ones with skeleton faces and rotting flesh dripping off them like wax in the sun, sweeping in on us like they were flying.

They were flying at us lieutenant. We barely let off any shots, they were so quick. Everyone panicked. Most of us dropped our rifles and started to run, tried to make it up the ridge. Men were putting pistols to their heads to end it right there. Hawkes screamed next to me, but I didn't see him 'cept his boots lifting up in the air, his blood raining down on me. They were demons, lieutenant.

I kept running, stumbling. Looking back, I saw they were on the ground, loping towards all of us who were trying to get away. They were like wolves the way they moved, but…once they were upon us they were more like men, dead men with long stringy hair and black pits for eyes.

They ripped men apart with claws and tore into them with jagged teeth. A group of men made it to a ravine only to be overtaken by a swarm of those things—they were all killed in an instant, but their screams dogged me like a shadow as I ran up the ridge toward the gray-red smoke where the guidon was planted. I saw Tom shoot the General in the head, then try to shoot himself, but one of the demons leaped on him, pinning him to the ground as it buried its fangs into his gut.

I got knocked to the ground. I expected to die. I wanted to die. It was all over. I saw the things, so thin now they looked like wisps of smoke, ravenous, scraping the meat off the bones with their teeth, feeding on us.

Franks slumped back with a sigh, drooling out of the side of his mouth, eyes closed.

"Not you, though," I said. I'd had enough. I was tired, hungry, terribly afraid, and I wanted to kill this worthless lying coward more than anything in the world.

Half Yellow Face was going to beat me to it. He lunged toward Franks with his knife drawn, just missing the man's throat. Godfrey knocked him to the side, giving the rest of us time to grab him. Half Yellow Face shouted something to Franks, who was laughing and crying at the same time. I looked to Lansing.

The interpreter said, "I'm not sure I understand. *Iya, Chiya-tanka, Bakaak.* Lakota words. All evil spirits or creatures. I think he is trying to come up with a name for the images Franks was talking about."

Half Yellow Face struggled. He was shaking, his face child-like as if he had just awakened from a nightmare and didn't know where he was. Half Yellow Face started to sing, and I knew it was the Crow death chant. He expected to die.

We let him go. He stood in the tent entrance. He spoke, directing his words to me.

"*Wetigo*," Lansing interpreted. "Plains Cree for Wendigo." Godfrey and I shook our heads. "It's an Indian evil spirit, very powerful. There are Wendigo legends in almost every tribe. They are like walking corpses with canine fangs—they feed on people and, the more they eat, the hungrier and more powerful they become." He paused. "If one is bitten by a Wendigo… they will go Wendigo."

Half Yellow Face started speaking again, a low secretive voice that carried just over the buzzing of the wretched flies.

"What's he saying?" I asked Lansing.

"*Wihtikowan*. There were many of them. They were called up by the big medicine in the village. They put a curse on you. On all of us."

When Lansing finished, Half Yellow Face pointed to Franks, then backed out of the tent and ran off.

"Fool," I said. I turned my attention back to Private Franks. We had saved his life a second time this day. I held Half Yellow Face's knife. The urge was still there to plunge it into this madman, but I needed to know what happened out there. "Franks," I said. "Finish."

"I want to eat," he croaked, thrashing so hard against the ropes that ribbons of blood splashed at us.

"He's finished," Godfrey said. "Leave the man in peace."

I leaned over Franks. Spasms of pain bolted up and down my arm. I knew it was infected. Damn him. "We'll get you food. Talk!"

"I played dead, but it didn't work. One of the fiends came to me and bit me in the arm. Shook me until I blacked out. Next thing I remember was the searing heat, and the godawful smell. There were voices all around me. And when I opened my eyes I saw Indians, squaws mostly, and old men, children, poking at the body parts, picking up anything they could use. Hats, clothes, weapons, they were taking everything. They shot arrows into bodies, slashed every piece of white man they could find. I waited for someone to notice me, but they stayed clear. I tried to crawl but couldn't move. I was a dead man. You know what they do to captives. I expected the worst.

"A squaw with a flat wizened face and a toothless grin came to me and kicked my leg, then moved away to other spoils. I closed my eyes. Heard them all around me, but they left me alone. I buried my head into my good arm and bit my sleeve to not cry out. I wanted to die."

Private Franks looked at us with his one good eye. His drawn-tight skin almost translucent, displaying his veins. We all knew what a dying man looked like. The doctor might take his arm, but it was already too late.

Franks wasn't going to make the steamer once it crawled to the mouth of the Little Bighorn to pick up the wounded.

I moved closer to him. "Every man with Custer was butchered, mutilated beyond recognition. You say you saw the squaws and old men plundering the battlefield, yet they left you alone, the only survivor? I know what the Sioux do with captives. You crawled in that horse and hid there during the heat of the battle while your comrades, *your friends*, fought and died. You're nothing but—"

"No! I didn't crawl into that horse!" Franks coughed and turned away. "They *put* me there. They put me in that damned horse!" He arched from the cot, struggling against the ropes that held him, sobbing and shaking. He tried to bite the ropes, snapping his jaws, then collapsed in on himself like a wrinkled gray blanket. He was done for the night.

Those of us left under Reno and Benteen's command kept to ourselves that night. We didn't talk. We avoided Terry's men, and they avoided us, somehow regarding us in disdain for having survived while Custer did not. I didn't think I could ever sleep again, the absence of stars in the night sky and the horrors of that battlefield too bright a light, like the whiteness you see through your eyelids when you look at the sun with closed eyes.

I was hungry, ravenously hungry. And the slightest touch on my arm sent spasms of pain throughout my body. I could hear men whimpering and crying, and then there was silence.

I was alone, walking the ridge where Custer lay. The dead were above the ground, bloated and blackened from the sun, but they were whole, unmutilated. The sun was cold and distant. I heard cries coming from the tall grass. The wet smell of death flowed into my nostrils. I stood over one of the slain troopers, his naked body glistening in the weak sun. I felt sick. Then a hunger I had never before experienced took hold. I tried to step back, watched my shadow retreat across the body like a swarm of flies interrupted in their feeding frenzy. I gagged and threw upon the dead trooper and tore at him with my teeth, ripping soft rancid strips of flesh to satisfy the incredible hunger overtaking me. The trooper's eyes, black spoiled pits, stared at me. The trooper screamed. I howled in hunger lust.

Shouts. I sprang from the ground, thankful to be finished with that awful, too-real dream. Now, screams. Fear paralyzed me. The taste of death still in my mouth as if I had eaten something putrid. I shook my head to wrench it away from the hideous dream. My first thought—we were under attack. The massive force of Indians that had laid siege to us for two days had returned.

I grabbed my Colt and stumbled into Lansing and Benteen. The screams were coming from the hospital tent. The three of us charged through the tent flaps expecting to see hostiles clubbing and hacking at our wounded.

It was far worse.

Franks had somehow broken free of his ropes. He was standing over one of our wounded, the man's throat torn apart, holding the man's arm to his face, gnawing the fingers like they were the tastiest delicacy in the wilderness. His blood-smeared face in ecstasy.

More men poured into the tent. As one we charged the thing that had once been Franks, grabbing his arms, keeping clear of his skull-like face, and the lipless mouth baring yellow fangs. He threw us about as if we were little children. Benteen managed to crack him across the jaw with his Colt, and someone hit him from behind with a rifle, finally dropping the man-beast to the ground. We dragged him outside, in disbelief that so emaciated a form could have been so strong.

We knew what we had to do. I didn't wait for an order. I put a bullet in Private Franks' brain. Benteen placed a hand on my shoulder and walked away.

In the morning Godfrey and I took him to the battlefield, where he should have died, and left him there in the open for the wolves and coyotes to eat. We knew that no man in the Seventh would ever speak of this, no man would ever let it be known that someone survived down there where Custer and his men fell. The idea would be as crazy as Franks' story of fantastic creatures called forth to annihilate the finest fighting force in the West. Or Half Yellow Face's belief that a curse was somehow unleashed on all of us.

—⚭—

We will be moving out soon. Porter put me in the field hospital, which had been moved to Gibbon's camp, a slightly cooler area near a creek bed. He says he will have to take my arm sometime today. Then I will be able to board the steamboat when it arrives, along with the other wounded. Some of the soldiers with me in this stinking tent will not be so lucky.

A blanket of flies eat at my arm which oozes pus. I am so hungry I lick at the flies.

"Private Franks" was the first time I had been invited to submit to an anthology. I knew I wanted to write a western horror story, and I remembered stories about the Battle of the Little Bighorn told to me from the Sioux perspective when I lived on the Rosebud Sioux Indian Reservation.

I added the supernatural elements, of course, but I tried to research the battle as carefully as possible while I wrote the story. The names in the story are authentic, and there was a man who supposedly survived the battle, at least by his account, a Crow Indian scout named Curly. His stories, which changed frequently over the years, were always suspect, but in one of them he survived the battle by crawling in and hiding in a dead horse while the battle took place.

Once I had that image in my head, the story took off. I took a lot of liberties, after all it is a horror story, and no one knows for sure how Custer met his end, but I certainly had fun with it. And it is obvious the many warriors involved in the battle didn't need any supernatural help to defeat the Seventh Cavalry that day.

All The Missing Things

Marianne could barely hear the words coming from his mouth, what with her ears boxed in and the blood-matted hair coiled over the right side of her head. Joseph ranting, words atop words dropping like a sorry waterfall, and she covered up best she could, waiting for the inevitable last kick. He left the room instead. Screaming at the walls. Moments like this were the worst. Sometimes he came back with a biblical fury to finish her off, sometimes he wound down easy and offered comfort words from a distant canyon, leaving her be, cold, wet, and dull. She never knew what to expect.

Joseph's words faded. A dim, tired light eased out of her.

Marianne stayed where she was until the rattles and bumps in the next room and beyond grew quiet. Her head throbbed. She drew quick, shallow breaths. She felt like she was deep under water, the pressure steady. It took some time to recover enough to roll over and brush her hair back and wipe the wetness from her eyes. She took slower breaths now and assessed the damage: just her ears and side of her head from falling against the table. Joseph didn't move in for the kill. Left her alone, probably left the house.

It was his way to cool off out in the yard. Maybe walk in the woods for an hour or two. He would come back with apologies if it had been especially bad or act as if nothing happened. Marianne ran her tongue against the back of her front teeth, unstuck some of the hair with numb fingers. She didn't read him right, not this time, when he couldn't find his glasses. Accused her of losing them. Just about tore the place up looking for them, then tore into her with empty hands.

"Feel what it's like not being able to see, bitch!" No, she didn't get that part, having her ears boxed instead of her eyes. Made no difference to him anyway. She supposed he gave up looking for the damned things, cheap brown turtle-framed readers with twisted scraps of masking tape holding them in one piece. They could've been anywhere, and she got all the blame. Couldn't read the paper now. From his high-pitched rants she caught, "... just one eye and you're trying to screw that one up!" and "...bad enough one eye was put out, then to have the other shrink to where I need glasses to see shit!"

Well. Can't read now. He can read the bushes and the tall weeds in the yard on the way to the woods. Marianne squeezed her eyes shut. The numbness now shook her brain. Standing up made her dizzy. She held onto the oak table, leaned over it, waited, listened. He was gone, for now.

The underwater pressure was gone too, replaced with a faint ringing that wafted a little every time she moved. The cut on the side of her head seemed to have clotted enough to stop bleeding freely but stung when she touched it. Joseph would return, and the glasses would still be gone, and she didn't want to be there in the kitchen, a place where his glasses usually were. She went to the bedroom. Turned the radio on. Talk stuff. Turned the radio off. Laid on the bed and pulled the covers up over her clothes and shut her eyes. Darkness.

He was on top of her. Then beside her. The musty earth smell of the basement. The smell of decay and mildew rising between them as they lay on the grass, no, not grass, a bed of worms growing around him like a cloak, holding him, entering him in all the places they could. She giggled hysterically as his screams became muffled from a worm-filled mouth. This Joseph was whole, the younger Joseph. But not for long. The worms, longer now, like sparkling electric wires, took him apart, bloodless but not painless, and each piece swallowed in the soupy earth as Marianne rolled herself in a ball and rested, still giggling, against a damp wall. Shadows that were once stars were her only comfort once he was gone.

The screen door slammed. Joseph called her name. Softly. He moved through the house in that plodding, shameful way of his and brushed his hand against the door like he was politely knocking, pushing it open as he did so. "Hon?" He slid to the side of the bed. Rubbed his calloused hand on her behind. "You know I go crazy when things get misplaced like that." He sucked in a long breath. "Can't do damned much around here without those glasses. My last pair, too. Can't believe two pair gone in one week."

She turned slightly. *Careful what you say.* "They have to be around here someplace." She didn't look at him. Didn't want to see that one eye blazing into her and the other, well, just there.

"I'll get another pair. Then they'll turn up." Joseph stood away from the bed.

She smelled perspiration and musk deodorant and maybe a trace of beer. *He must've gotten off work early and stopped somewhere.*

Joseph rummaged through the end table drawer. "Damn, my watch is missing too. Maybe I left it at the factory."

"You going now?" she asked. Her eyes open to the window and the growing darkness. A wasp batted against the glass. A cool breeze settled in through the screen. She could feel him shaking his head behind her, moving to the doorway, then lingering there.

"Sorry 'bout what I done," he said. "It's just…you give me that look, you know, sets me off. Like you always know something more'n you're letting on."

Marianne shivered, even under the covers. She didn't turn to face him while he stood in the doorway.

"I didn't mean to hurt you," he continued. "Lord knows I love you to death." He turned away and went into the hall. "I should've known better. I need you, more than anything."

Joseph inched out of the house. In twenty breaths the car roared out of the driveway and onto the road that hid behind their front trees. Marianne smiled. Squeezed the man's sorry glasses in her fist beneath the pillow. He was losing everything.

———⁓———

Joseph was right, of course. He had no one else, even though he pretended he had friends. She was all he had in the world, and he was determined to make sure he was all she had, as well.

When she left school to work at the knife factory it was Joseph—tall, lanky, and crude— who caught her eye. He was the one who could deliver her from her crazy family and the dull job at the factory. He was the one. Joseph wanted her, and that was enough. He wanted her all to himself, so when they married she quit her job and devoted her time to making him happy. She stopped seeing her family and friends, all of them disapproving of this older and controlling man. They moved to a place far out in the country. The only times Marianne went into town, or saw anyone, she was with him. She was fine with that.

Everything changed when she became pregnant.

———⁓———

It was getting dark. Marianne went to the bedroom window and looked out. Watched the twins playing by the swing on the old oak. Little Jonathan twisted the swing around after Jessie climbed aboard. Marianne placed her hand on the screen and listened to bits of laughter falling with the leaves in the breeze. Their long blond hair ablaze. Her fingers traced the screen where their images were, then pressed harder, wanting to be there with them in the yard. Jesse screamed in delight as the swing spun around. Jonathan turned and looked toward the window with shadowy orbs where eyes used to be, his melting features more bleached bone than skin now, and grinned.

She loved his smile.

The phone rang. And rang. Marianne scuttled downstairs to the kitchen where the wall phone was and picked it up on the seventh or eighth ring.

"You okay?" Joseph asked. "It took a while for you to answer the phone."

She swallowed. "I'm...I'm fine. I must've dozed off."

"Well, go back to sleep then. Just checking to see how you're doing." He paused, his breathing heavy on the phone. She could make out commotion in the background and wondered how long he'd be at the bar.

"Did you find your watch?" she asked.

"No." He hung up. She stared at the receiver in her hand before dropping it. Watched the tight phone cord unwind rapidly until it rested on the floor. Like Jesse spinning on the swing moments earlier.

She debated leaving it there, then went ahead and hung up the phone. Joseph called her twenty times a day, at least. She paced back and forth in the kitchen wringing her hands. She tried to think of a time when she loved the man and realized she probably never did. Tried to think of a time when she didn't hate the man, realized she couldn't.

Marianne went back upstairs, rummaged through his things in the dresser, and pulled out an envelope with his car title and some insurance papers inside. She folded the envelope and took it along with his reading glasses and watch down to the kitchen.

—∞—

"Hon, do you know where the coffee is?" Joseph had just about ripped the cabinet doors off their hinges, a tired, defeated expression painted where his face should have been. Out all night. Reeked of alcohol.

Marianne stood in the kitchen doorway in her red robe and bare feet shaking her head.

He glared at her for a second. Then stared at the empty Mr. Coffee. "I know we bought some coffee the other day."

"I don't drink coffee. I wouldn't pay attention if we bought it or not. And you're the one who makes it, once in a blue moon. Don't you remember where you put it?"

"Look. I know you're still mad about the way I treated you last night. I can be a real prick sometimes, especially when I lose shit." She cringed and he noticed it. "You're not thinking about leaving, are you?"

"I got nowhere to go."

"Damn straight." He walked to the door. Bent down and pulled his jeans up enough to show his prosthetic leg, then lifted it in her direction like he was stretching before a run. "You should be grateful I don't lock you up no more," he said, smiling. "Guess I'll pick up some coffee at McDonalds." He left without another word.

—✺—

When Joseph came home from the hospital after the terrible accident, he was a broken man left with wispy scars and only memories of being whole. He started locking Marianne in the cellar. This was after her mom died from a stroke and she had wanted to go to the funeral. Joseph would have none of that, afraid she would leave him with her mom gone and all.

Every morning before leaving for work he would drag her down the steps to the cellar and lock the door. There were no windows in the cellar. The only light a bare bulb suspended by a cord. She screamed against the cool concrete walls and cried and clawed to get out, but it didn't help. She peed and shat where the floor gave way to earth. She sat in the dark until he came home in the early evening to let her out. She would run to the babies' room and throw herself on the floor where their cribs used to be, turn herself into a wall of bricks, motionless until one by one the bricks loosened and crumbled. In time she found herself in the kitchen cooking the man his late supper.

Marianne thought of escape, then over time didn't think about it anymore. Easy enough to run from a one-eyed, one-legged man, but he was right, there was no place to go after her mom died. After a few years he stopped taking her down to the cellar. She went down there anyway. It was her place, now, and she grew to love the dampness, the rich earth smells, the things that skittered and spun and danced on microscopic highways across the walls and spaces between. No, she wasn't going anywhere.

—✺—

Marianne watched Joseph leave. Caught the top of the car as it passed by the kitchen window, then she crossed over to the garbage can by the fridge and pulled out a bag of coffee from underneath the plastic garbage bag. She opened the coffee bag and smelled the bitter aroma of dark roast before spotting the brown turtle-frame glasses poking out from the grounds, along with part of a wadded envelope. A silver piece of watchband gleamed in the light. She carried the bag to the cellar door, hesitated, looked behind her to make sure he was really gone, then went down the narrow steps.

The cellar was dark even with the hanging light bulb. Marianne liked that. The rough concrete floor gave way to earth after about fifteen feet. The concrete was cool to her feet. When she crossed to the dirt the effect was simple and soothing. Marianne went to her spot in the corner, the darkest corner.

Tiny white straw-like fingers waved and fluttered as if moved by the slightest hint of a breeze. Only there was no breeze. There were hundreds of the things now. Brought forth from the earth, living confetti, always hungry. Marianne fed them the coffee grounds, the glasses, the watch, then the envelope and empty bag. She sat on the earthen floor and watched as all the items dissolved into a boiling liquid and hissed, and then a noxious low cloud, all of it inhaled, sucked by the tubes frantic to each get a piece of the gaseous remains.

Marianne relaxed and smiled. "Now babies," she said, "let's remember to share."

———※———

The first time she saw the finger-worms, as she liked to call them, was after a beating for giving a store clerk undue attention when he helped her with some dropped groceries in the market, Joseph seeing them both bent down in the aisle looking at each other.

He didn't let on he was mad until they were home, and then he gave it to her good. "Can't stand another man looking at you, babe. Do you have to fucking look back at em?" He later apologized. "Just love you too much."

After he left for work the next day Marianne retreated to the cellar, her prison for so long, now a safe comfortable place away from him. She found the soft spot in the far corner, the sacred place, where she had wept so often for her babies that had been taken from her. This was their home, their precious home forever, the two of them buried deep by Joseph the day she miscarried.

Marianne had brought down Joseph's high school ring and a pair of his favorite socks and buried them in the sacred spot, knowing it would drive him batshit crazy looking for them once he realized they were missing. She drew herself up on her haunches, tucked her head in, and strained to hear the padding of little feet upstairs. All she heard was the distant drip of the kitchen faucet.

The following day she again went down to the sacred spot in the cellar. Delicate white spaghetti-like things eased from the ground where she had buried the ring and socks. She thought, at first, that they were a kind of fungi or a type of grass that had adapted to the world of shadows. Little tubes, almost translucent. They were several inches high and trembled as if soaking up every vibration from her heart. In her hands was one of his favorite belts and his favorite black comb, which she intended to bury. She tossed them onto the patch of fluttering tubes. Immediately the tubes reacted, whipping the items into a frothy goo before greedily sucking it away.

Marianne fell back in awe. "What are you?" she asked.

The tubes rippled and swayed, and she thought there were even more of them now than before, but that was crazy. She ran upstairs. She was not crazy. She was not.

—⚌—

That was several months ago. The finger-worms were bigger and hungrier than when she'd first seen them. She didn't know what they were, but she was convinced they had something to do with her babies, her lost babies.

It was a beating that caused the miscarriage. Joseph refused to take her to the hospital. When she eventually recovered, he showed her the place in the cellar where the babies were buried. She gave them names, Jessie and Jonathan, and visited the spot in the cellar almost every day. It was the sacred spot.

Months after the miscarriage she saw the two of them in the yard. They were older, still babies in her eyes but big enough to play independently. She knew they belonged to her the instant she saw them.

When she burst from the back door in a frenzy of fear and relief they were gone as if they had never been there. She knew they would return. She was not crazy. She was not. The children wanted her to see them, but it was not okay to get too close. They might be hallucinations but on *their* terms.

She saw the children infrequently. Often when she least expected it. Usually in the yard. Sometimes a flash from the corner of her eye if she dared to open the little room that would have been theirs. Every time she saw them, they seemed to be growing a little older yet decaying at the same time, losing their flesh. She didn't mind. They were her babies. She never told Joseph.

—⚌—

It wasn't too long after she first started seeing the twins that she discovered the finger-worms. She knew the things were connected to her children, somehow. Every time she went down into the cellar the finger worms appeared to have been waiting for her, expecting to be fed. They reminded her of baby chicks in a nest, with their mouths open, always hungry. Marianne thought they were beautiful. There was almost a glow to them, like luminescent creatures beneath the sea. Swaying with the currents. If the finger-worms were part of something bigger, something born of her children, then there was no way she could ever neglect them.

She tried giving the finger-worms different things. Day-old tuna salad, untouched. One of her scarves, untouched. Carrots. Wooden utensils. A pair of her socks. All met with agitated indifference. Joseph's pipe tobacco. The fingers went at it like manna from heaven. She fed them the pipe, then one of his favorite screwdrivers, an old worn one he preferred to use. The metal and plastic and wood danced in a frenzy of tethering mouths, and she noticed a faint glow like dimming Christmas lights. Satisfaction.

It must be something of his, something he needs. She smiled. She hadn't smiled in a long time.

Marianne visited the cellar every day. Took something of his to feed the hungry mouths waiting for her. Always things he cherished or needed. Sometimes when she searched the house for things to take she would catch a glimpse of the twins playing in the yard or peeking around a corner in the hallway. Skeletal figures with long blond hair and irrepressible grins. On these occasions Marianne collected as many of his things as she could carry, a feast for the finger-worms.

The finger-worms slowly but steadily grew. Now they were at pencil height, about as thick as a child's finger. They nodded and quivered when she approached them. She fed them one of Joseph's track medals from high school. He could run fast, once, back when he had two legs. Fed them his pocketknife from when he was a little boy. His car keys. He went berserk losing them, she had bruises for a week.

As long as it belonged to Joseph the finger-worms went at it aggressively. When they were finished there was nothing left, only a slight hissing noise like the aftermath of a fire. Marianne didn't dwell on what they were or where they came from. She only knew they had something to do with the twins. And in the end, it was worth the beatings and verbal tirades to slowly take away pieces of Joseph's life.

—ᵂ—

"Honey? Have you seen my eye?" Joseph asked.

"No, I haven't seen it."

"I coulda' sworn I left it on the nightstand."

"You look under the bed? It could've rolled off."

"I looked under the bed. I checked every square inch of the floor, under the dresser, everywhere."

"It could've rolled pretty far. The hallway?"

"Hell, I looked in the hallway, too. Checked the kitchen." He stared at her hard with his one eye, red and agitated, paused a few beats and then said, "In case you asked, I checked there."

Marianne wanted to smile. Knew better. Painted concern and worry all over her face as best she could. "You were pretty lit up last night, Joseph. Sure you brought it home?"

He thought about that. The creases around his mouth turned and scrunched up like he had to hold back vomit. He sometimes pulled the eye out when he was at the bar for amusement, if he was drunk enough. This was going to put him in a pissy mood. "Guess I'll wear the eye patch, then. 'Til it turns up." He pulled back his arm like he was going to swing at her, shook his head instead. He had to get to work. It could wait.

"I'll look for it," she said.

"Yeah, you do that." His eye bored into her. Damned if he wasn't going crazy. The look he gave her said, *I know you know something.*

Joseph stormed out of the house. She heard the Firebird crunch gravel and spin away. Yeah, his day will start off sour. She pictured him at the factory, limping around with his fake leg and eye patch like a silly pirate. He might just run out of body parts at this rate.

—∞—

The finger-worms took special pleasure with the glass eye. They passed it around before the tubes stuck into it from all directions and sucked away in a glass-popping and melting frenzy.

"My babies," Marianne said, sitting on the cool concrete, a cool distance away. She didn't know what would happen if she touched the finger-worms accidentally or on purpose. Well, she thought, she *might* know. It wouldn't be pretty.

She spent more and more time in the cellar now, whenever Joseph was out of the house. She hadn't seen the twins in a while.

"My baby's fingers," she said over and over. Chanting. Marianne watched the finger-worms' delicate dance, figured they were dancing for her, and when she was upstairs, they were always waiting, always hungry. She had been feeding them for months, but she was painting herself into a corner. The more things that Joseph missed, the more he tightened his stranglehold on her. He called her constantly to make sure she was still there. When he was home, he didn't let her out of his sight.

And she was positive he suspected her of taking his things.

If she left him, he would have nothing, and he knew it. He couldn't allow that to happen. Joseph would surely kill her like he did the twins.

Whatever the finger-worms were, they glowed in appreciation whenever their meal was finished. She thought they would start on the house itself if she ran out of his things, or if she simply left them alone. It wasn't enough to take him apart piece by piece, memory by memory, feeding the pieces to whatever they were. At least he rarely went to the cellar, and when he did it was to attend to the furnace at the other end. He never went to the earth section.

A light began to crawl around the back of her head. So faint, at first, she almost missed it. Then she caught it and drew it toward her. The fingers never left a trace of anything they feasted on. Where it all went, she had no idea, didn't really want to know. *Joseph.*

The phone rang. It rang eight times before she got upstairs to the kitchen, out of breath and hardly able to make a hesitant hello. Joseph grumbled something about making him wait so long to hear her fucking voice then hung up. She looked forward to not having to answer the phone again.

—⁓—

"I know where your leg is." Marianne said, standing by the steps leading to the cellar. Joseph had been asleep on the couch in the living room. When he awoke the prosthetic leg was gone. He struggled up and hopped to the closet door to get the crutches.

"You're fucking with me. I ain't in the fucking mood. Where's my goddamned leg?" Marianne flipped the light switch and started down into the cellar, her bare feet sucking at the wooden steps. "What the hell?"

"Come on," she said. "Down here."

Of course, he knew she had been taking his things. He let the anger build up, sometimes letting a little vent out, but this was the fucking last straw. And the cellar. He hated the cellar—it was her prison, not his. *His things*. Probably piled in a corner somewhere. He wondered how she'd take a crutch to the side of the head. Dent up that pretty face.

Joseph took a deep breath. Put the crutches out front and took the steps, one at a time. Okay. Maybe he wouldn't hit her right off. Maybe she could give him an explanation. He treated her good. She couldn't do better than him, he made sure of that. Hell, he didn't lock her up down there anymore, right? The crutches creaked, and his good leg stomped onto the concrete floor. The bitch was at the far end of the cellar, in the dim shadows beyond the floor.

"I know where all your missing things are," she said.

He squinted. Hopped up to her with the crutches. Supported himself with one and lifted the other like he was going to swing it. But he didn't. She was kneeling by the funniest-looking shit he had ever seen, growing out of the dirt.

"What the hell is that?" It had to be some kind of fungi, but he never saw anything like that waving and fluttering about, and yet there was no draft, no cause for them to be moving the way they did.

"Your things," Marianne said, motioning toward the fungi-like things. They glowed. They pulsed. Throbs of dull light. Joseph was transfixed. He leaned forward, setting the crutches aside, lowering himself to get a better look. Took his eye off Marianne. Shook his head. Weird, was what it was. Better get an exterminator in here.

"These are my babies. I call them finger-worms because they look so much like little fingers. I think they belong to Jesse and Jonathan."

"What? Where's my shit? What the fuck are you…" Something heaved into him from behind, knocking him forward, and the next thing he knew he was in the things and the dirt. They tickled where they touched his bare skin. Then a burning sensation. Thousands of pinpricks. He blacked out, but only for a second. He came to, sunken in the earth and the crushed-down fungi things which now felt like soft feathers, like newly sprouted grass, and memories drifting just out of reach, drifting away…

"Damn!" Joseph pushed himself up, crawled backwards crablike out of the mass of shivering white. "Whadja do that for? I'm all muddy and wet!" He shut his eye. Somewhere, in the far distance outside, he heard the faint sound of children playing and laughing. Something was wrong. It was more than shock. Kind of like the first time he woke in the hospital after the car accident, only this time parts of him were leaking away, all his memories, everything that made him who he was, all of it leaving in a dizzying rush. *My name, my name.* Just out of reach, just like the woman standing over him.

He was becoming empty. He could feel it, his self, leaking out as sure as the blood would flow if he had slit his wrists.

The woman before him stood frozen. A look of disbelief on her face, staring at the white stalks he had crawled from. He was covered in dirt and naked, all his clothes, belt, wedding ring, everything, gone. The woman. Who was this woman? Someone he needed. Someone he felt intense anger towards.

He pushed himself up, standing on one leg, and grabbed both her arms. "Here, see what it feels like." He flung her into the tubes and the dirt, and before he could even turn, she was screaming and splintering apart. The things rose and all of them were on her and in her. Writhing, more tentacles now than tubes, tethering her to the frothy ground. She struggled, screams shattering the walls and ceiling. Her clothes and skin melted and sputtered as if she were on a buttered griddle.

He pulled at her arms, but it was like trying to hold onto water. She slipped away. The screaming withered, and what was left of her body thrashed once as a single glowing string erupted from her mouth, swung around, and stabbed into one of her eye puddles. There was a wet slurping sound.

The man fell back. Screamed. Slapped at the red and yellow puddle that was once a person, chips of bones popping and crackling and eager, hungry tendrils sucking every drop with a ferocity that pulled him forward, into the vortex of liquid earth and tentacles and scent crumbs of someone he used to know. He ripped at them, but they dissolved sinking into the earth dancing in effervescent light.

He clawed and scratched, buried his head into the dirt, soft and wet where wisps of white remained fog-like and ethereal. He had to get her back. Whoever she was. He had to dig and dig, without stopping, find her, find everything the earth had just taken, just keep digging, even as everything inside him was being chipped away. The laughter and shouts from children much closer, maybe behind him, but he didn't turn to look. He had to keep at it, digging until the skin and muscle were flayed to the bone, and he would keep digging until there was nothing left.

Nothing.

"All the Missing Things" is one of my earlier stories. It was never published although it was short-listed a few times. One nice rejection email from a well-known podcast stated that they really liked the story but after long consideration felt that it was too controversial (domestic abuse) for them to want to deal with.

The story idea at first was simply an abused wife who steals and hides her husband's things. It eventually morphed into a horror story with supernatural elements and perhaps some cosmic horror elements as well. I liked the concept of children who died but seemed to grow in the afterlife, and I wanted to be vague about what the feathery finger-worms were—they were connected to the children in some way, but what was really growing from that spot?

Poem Of The Riverbank

Originally published in Todd Sullivan Presents:
The Vampire Connoisseur *by Nightmare Press, 2020*

Seven miles south of Denver, along Cherry Creek, a tired man with a full pack on his back and walking stick in his hand rested on a slab of concrete beneath an underpass. It was dark but slivers of light crept through at either end. The man listened to the unraveling of the water as it rushed to the rapids not more than twenty feet away. It was a bogus moon, the man thought, as he leaned away from the ball of light that flittered toward him, soft and fragile like Chinese lanterns he'd seen somewhere a long time ago. The bogus moon grew dark and large and stopped near the man in the swift but shallow water.

The tired man stood and gripped his stick like a baseball bat, ready to swing with all the might his beaten sixty-year-old body could muster. He started to speak but before he could the light reached out to his throat, filling it with mud and river slime, a swelling fist forcing its way gently but forcefully, crushing his trachea and esophagus, his eyes suddenly on the trail of stars and the real moon as he was dragged into the water and out of the underpass. His last thought was how pretty the watermelon moon was.

—⚏—

Gerald woke early, as usual. The sun was morning dull. It was exactly seven o'clock. He removed and folded his pajamas neatly and placed them in the dresser, then put on gray sweatpants and a gray tee shirt. He brushed his teeth a full sixty seconds, gargled with mouthwash, then wiped the mirror where splashes of water and toothpaste had landed. He used the toilet, washed his hands and face, and brushed his hair. He donned a gray sweatshirt before leaving for the river.

The South Platte River was two and a half blocks from his one-bedroom apartment in downtown Denver. A path led to the riverbank not far from a pedestrian bridge, and Gerald followed it until he came to a bench that faced the river. In late fall and winter, when the trees were bare, he could see the skyline of the city, and he always enjoyed watching the soft rushing water of the river. At night he sat on the bench and listened to it bubble past.

Gerald said hello to everyone he met on the path. He liked people. All people, whether they crawled out from the bushes reeking of body odor and alcohol and pot or walked on the path wearing a Polo outfit and top-end running shoes. He noticed shoes. Make and model, how they were worn, how the person carried themselves in the shoes. He was a shoe salesman, after all.

"You can tell a lot about a person the way they walk or run in their shoes," he told a homeless man named the Sage that morning. The Sage didn't talk much but often met Gerald at the bench around sunup. Gerald paid attention to him and talked to him like he was a normal person. The Sage liked that. Besides, Gerald enjoyed Edgar Allan Poe as much as he did, and they often shared bits and pieces of the man's writings between them.

"And by the kind of shoes they're wearing." Gerald pointed to two young women walking the trail. "See, that lady's toes are going off her sandals. She needs to loosen up. And her friend's trying to impress everybody, but her cheap Adidas are wearing out on the sides."

Gerald regarded the Sage's boots, worn out, no determinable brand. "I keep telling you, come into Macy's and I'll find you some good boots. No charge. You shouldn't wear those worn-out things."

The Sage followed the early morning clouds, nodded. "You need more friends."

"Tell you what," Gerald said. "I'll pick up a pair for you." He studied the Sage's boots. "Looks like you wear a size ten."

"Shoes are fine," the Sage said. He was a short man with a droopy face, layers of clothes and coats that gave him a Quasimodo look. "Be careful, my friend. Word is out that a maniac is butchering people on the trails. Everyone's scared shitless." He shook his head. "*Sir, said I, or madam, truly your forgiveness I implore...*'" He bowed and swept his greasy hands before him. "'*But the fact is I was napping, and so gently you came tapping...*'"

He slowly pushed his cart, overflowing with unnecessary things. "'*Tap-*

ping at my chamber door, that I scarce was sure I heard you.'" With a broad half-toothed smile, he ambled off along the riverbank.

Gerald shouted, *"'Here I opened wide the door—Darkness there, and nothing more!'"*

The Sage cackled with laughter, and, without turning, gave a subtle wave goodbye. Gerald watched him go. Followed the current of the water. Noted the branches and man-made debris float by. The water was high. It was early spring and the trees opposite were blooming white, some of the branches stripped of flowers by the rain the night before. Petals floated by like mad teacups.

—m—

Gerald worked at Macy's in the men's shoe department. Business had been slow and usually he was the only salesman on duty. He worked from 11:00 am to 9:00 pm every day except Thursday and Sunday. He thought of the customers who visited the store as friends, or people who could become friends.

That night Mr. Barnes bought a pair of Hushpuppy loafers. Mr. Barnes was a friend. He reminisced about trips he had taken with his late wife. Gerald had never been out of Colorado before and was keenly interested in what Mr. Barnes said. He had read about many distant places and desperately wanted to see the rest of the world. But he knew he never would. Mr. Barnes was a lucky man indeed. Gerald said so. Mr. Barnes didn't appear to appreciate the remark and left the store soon after.

Mr. and Mrs. Johnson, a nice elderly couple who lived in a high-rise not far from Gerald, also came in and bought walking shoes. Mrs. Johnson had recently been diagnosed with cancer, and after they left Gerald was quiet with worry.

As he was straightening the boxes strewn on the floor, he overheard Mrs. Warstein, who worked in the women's clothing department, and Ted, a young college student who worked part-time evenings, talking about a gruesome discovery along Cherry Creek that some bicyclists stumbled upon that day. Mrs. Warstein was upset about it, this being the third homicide in Denver that month along one of the waterways. Gerald wanted to hear more details, but was sidetracked when two young men came over, looking for running shoes.

The odor of marijuana was strong, and the kids were beside themselves with the way Gerald waited on them. They giggled and almost rolled off the chairs with every polite thing he said, and when Gerald turned his back, they mocked everything he did and said. Gerald thanked them effusively for shopping at Macy's and for giving him the pleasure of waiting on them. When he said, "Have a great evening!" they shouted "Have a great evening!" back to him, over and over, all the way through the store and out into the mall. Ted and Mrs. Warstein laughed, but Gerald didn't mind. The kids bought shoes, and Gerald felt he gave good customer service.

He was thinking about the homicides when a dark-dressed stranger came in looking for wingtips shortly before closing. He was old, a weathered face held together with fine lines, like minute cracks in antique porcelain, and was very thin. He moved like he weighed nothing at all.

Gerald said hello and told the man that he looked distinguished, getting a chuckle from the man. Gerald commented on the man's accent.

"Armenian," the man said.

Gerald placed a handful of shoe boxes before the customer, knelt down to slip off the man's well-worn but expensively made shoe. The shoe tingled his fingers. Static electricity, he thought.

"We don't carry anything quite like these," Gerald said. "But the Florsheim is good. Let's see how they fit." The shoe was tight. "Armenia. I've read about that country. I've always been interested in geography." He stood. "Let me check and see if we have a larger size."

He went into the backroom and returned shortly after. "I'm sorry," he said. He looked straight into the man's murky blue eyes. Distant eyes, ocean deep. "I can order them from one of our other stores. They'll be here tomorrow."

"That will be fine." The man crossed his legs, content to stay awhile. "Have you worked here long?"

"I've been here forever," Gerald said. "I practically live here." He sat on the stool before the man, still fixed on those eyes. He asked if the man lived around here, he seemed new to these parts.

"You're observant," the man said. His long white hair reached his shoulder but was impeccably well-placed without appearing overly fashioned. "I'm new to Denver. I moved here from the coast." He went on to say how different it was compared to New York, the people more relaxed, nicer even, and the wide-open spaces.

They talked until closing time. Gerald was polite and conversational to a fault. He loved meeting new customers and hearing their stories.

The man asked about him, where he lived, what he did when he was off work. Gerald said the store was his life, but he did like to spend time by the river. Water was magical.

"Indeed, it is," the man said.

The man stood and extended his hand. Gerald took it although he rarely liked to touch people. The man's grip was surprisingly soft and cool. "Arsen," the man said. "I enjoyed talking with you."

"I'm Gerald. Your shoes will be here tomorrow night, Arsen." He paused. "I'll be here."

—⁂—

The Sage stumbled on the trail, caught himself with the aid of a dead tree branch that scratched his hand, and returned upright and unsteady. He wiped his hand on a blanket in his cart then pushed ahead down the narrow trail. The wind kicked up and scattered leaves and paper trash like ice feathers dropped from the heavens.

The Sage breathed heavy. He was tired and a little drunk and a lot cold, the wind slipping into every hole his clothes allowed. He cursed the night. He cursed the assholes who took his spot a mile down the river—his home, by God, the Sage's kingdom—and there he was, in the middle of the night in the dark, listening to the running water and the cackle of wind pushing against the trees and shrubbery.

Then a soft voice. "'*From childhood's hour I have not been, as others were—I have not seen, as others saw…*'"

"Gerald, is that you?" The Sage stumbled off the path into the weeds where he thought the voice had come from.

He never heard the scythe-like claws that ripped into and through his neck. Before he could gargle out a blood soaked cry he was falling back, and something was on him, something monstrous big. Crushing his chest, the bones crackling like a bonfire. The Sage didn't feel the teeth on his ripped throat, many teeth, gnashing and tearing to get at what life force flowed out. Somewhere way distant he thought a large cat, a mountain lion, had got him.

Then a sigh. No, it was the air escaping from his severed windpipe. And when all the blood and air were siphoned from his body, and he knew he was dead, he heard, "'*And all I lov'd, I lov'd alone.*'"

A dark shape hovered over the body and pulled pieces of it apart, as if the Sage had been made of malleable clay. The pieces were scattered along the weeds and the easy river. The shape wiped the blood from its mouth with an arm that reached to the ground. It wobbled slightly from the gorging it had just taken.

A cloud uncovered part of the moon, and light rippled on the surface of the river. The banks on both sides were overgrown with lush plant life, and there should have been the sound of crickets, cicadas, mosquitos' wings, and frogs, mournful wails of night birds, the fervent rustling of rodents, but there was no sound whatsoever. The dark shape was accustomed to the silence of nature, and, buried deep in some ancient memory, missed those sounds.

The running water was soothing, and the shape took in the neon reflections of the moon on the water's surface. The river was the source of all life, of all death. Things never changed over countless centuries and new lands.

It could have walked the city streets, the many dark alleys, the secluded parks, the hallways of near-empty office buildings to find nourishment, and sometimes it did. Sometimes it made a game of the hunt, selecting and seizing its prey in the most open of places, sometimes even in a crowd or well-lit department store. It was a magician at disposing bodies.

But the shape preferred waterways, whether they be rivers, creeks, or canals. For centuries it could simply follow the river and select prey and never worry about the monotony of returning to the same scene. It could move great distances and always have reliable sources of food. The river, rich in symbolism, the birthplace of all great civilizations, the arteries and veins of the planet.

The creature turned within itself and became a shadow that swallowed the night whole and disappeared.

The Sage's cart took the first sprinkles of a light rain, and then the steady downpour on the side of the dirt path, the front wheels buried in weeds and mud and only yards from the closest pieces of what was left of the Sage.

—⚬—

In the morning, when Gerald left his apartment to visit the river, he discovered an envelope by his door. He assumed a neighbor or the apartment manager put it there since the building had a locked entry. Nothing was written on it, but there was something hard inside. He opened it.

He immediately gasped and dropped the envelope to the floor as if it had ignited in his hands. A severed finger, gray, bloodless, and desiccated. He pulled himself together and picked it up, studied it for a second until he became nauseous, dropped it again. His first thought was to call the police. Then the apartment manager. He thought on it, hard.

People in the building were always teasing him. It *had* to be a practical joke. *Well. I'm not going to give them any satisfaction.* He dropped it in the dumpster on the way to his usual spot near the river.

—⚬—

He was out of sorts all day but didn't want to tell anyone about what he'd found that morning. And it bothered him that he didn't see his friend, the Sage. He tried to busy himself with straightening shoeboxes in the back-room, and every time he peeked out from the curtain all he saw was Mrs. Warstein pacing about. She was angry that Ted didn't show up that evening without calling in.

Then, about an hour before closing, Gerald saw Arsen standing by a rack of shoes. Gerald came out of the backroom and smiled as he brought a shoebox from beneath the register. To Gerald, the tall man seemed different than the night before when he appeared gaunt and chalk white. Now his cheeks were flushed as if he had been exposed to a harsh mountain wind.

"Hello, Arsen," Gerald said.

The man's eyes narrowed, cut a swath through Gerald as if he could best be examined in separate pieces. Then his thin lips parted and spread into a warm smile like that between friends seeing each other after being separated for a long time.

"Gerald," he said, placing both porcelain hands on the counter and leaning forward. His breath was mint-flavored, although Gerald picked up traces of fresh-tilled earth, the effect being like smelling mint leaves stripped from the plant and resting in rich soil.

"Shoes came in today, like I said they would." He came around from behind the counter and handed the box to Arsen. "Let's try them on, see how they fit."

The shoes fit perfectly. Arsen walked with ease on the carpeted floor. He swiveled on his feet like Fred Astaire, light and graceful. Gerald commented that he reminded him of the great dancer. Arsen said he appreciated that, he admired the man and had seen all his movies.

"The store is almost empty," Arsen said. His narrowed eyes followed Mrs. Warstein as she wandered about, moving behind one display and out another. A young couple walked by carrying bags.

"It's almost closing time," Gerald said, "But please, don't hurry. Take your time deciding on the shoes."

"They're fine. I'll take them."

"If there's any problem, anything at all, you bring them back and I'll take care of it."

"You're very passionate about your work," Arsen said. "That's unusual these days."

"I like to make people happy."

Arsen smiled. "We are simple creatures at heart. In such a complicated world. Forgive me if I am bold—are you married, do you have a significant other, as they say?"

Gerald's attempt at a smile turned to a swallow. "No. I live alone." He tried not to look at Arsen's face. "I like living alone. I can do what I want."

"I live alone, too."

"Sometimes it can be scary, living where I do, near the river. You heard about the body that was mutilated several miles away near Cherry Creek?" He almost mentioned the finger he found that morning but decided against it.

"I heard about it."

"Awful. The poor homeless man." They stood by the register. Arsen paid cash. "I talk to fellows like him all the time when I go to the river. Most of them are good people. Sometimes they help me pick up trash along the riverbank."

"The river can be a dangerous place. Especially at night. Death lurks behind every dark corner."

"There are no corners on a river," Gerald said. "But there are bad places and bad people."

Arsen laughed. "You are a poem, Gerald. There is great power in such simplicity and conciseness. I enjoyed this time with you."

—⚡—

Two young women finished their late-night McDonalds hamburgers while they walked on the trail along the Platte River. They balled up the wrappers and bags and casually tossed them into the wooded area that bordered the river, laughing. One said it was food for the homeless. The other said they needed to feed the serial killer terrorizing the city. They stopped when they noticed how quiet the woods had become, and before either could say a word, a shadow enveloped and lifted them both to a high tree limb, breaking their necks in the process. The shadow drained the bodies of fluids, then ripped each one apart piece by piece, painstakingly slow, dropping the body parts along the base of the tree.

It planted the legs in the wet muddy bank of the river, pushing the feet to mid-calf, the result looking like pale, shriveled stalks of exotic plants. The shadow impaled the arms on tree limbs. Christmas ornaments. The trunk and head of one woman was tossed into the river to be carried by the current, until it snagged on a rock or submerged tree. It forced the other woman's head and trunk into a small container for dog waste by the trail. It was a tight fit and the metal bulged almost to bursting, but the shadow made it fit. The body, devoid of fluids and the bones pulverized, squished into the container the way a tent would be packed in a rucksack.

The shadow rested in a tree, weightless on the light branches, then retrieved the litter left by the women and disposed of it in the same container that held the woman's remains.

It picked out each distinct smell in the area. There were millions. Then it concentrated on distant sounds, since all animal life was silenced in the immediate area. The soft padding of lovers walking on a sidewalk. Someone rustling about in a makeshift tent somewhere upriver. People moving and jostling in their safe beds in nearby apartments. Cars rumbling and exhausting the night air, metal garbage cans in alleyways banging about, the scratch of paper blown along highways, drunks rambling and cursing, and somewhere, flesh pounding in a fistfight.

The smells and sounds came together all at once, and even with this sensory symphony it still heard thousands of heartbeats and smelled the blood pulsing through miles of arteries and veins.

The shadow floated upwards and blended with the wet-laced wind, leaving no trace of its existence save the remains of its dinner.

—⚬⚬⚬—

Arsen visited the store every night that week. He arrived at about the same time, an hour before closing and sat in the same chair. Gerald often sat next to him. Business was slow and Gerald welcomed the company of a man he was intrigued with. He was pleased that Arsen wore the shoes he purchased.

"You don't mind me stopping by, do you?" Arsen asked.

"Oh no," Gerald said. "I enjoy hearing about the places where you lived and visited."

Arsen told him about Armenia, Turkey, Greece, Russia, Portugal, Spain, Hungary, Yugoslavia, Germany, and many more. He had been just about everywhere in Europe and the Middle East. He talked about the beautiful rivers in Europe: the Volga, the Rhine, the Don, the Elbe.

"I love rivers, any kind of waterway, really," Gerald said, fascinated. He fired off question after question. He couldn't get over how much Arsen had gotten around. "I've never left Colorado, have hardly been out of Denver." Arsen shook his head. "But I read a lot."

He shared with Arsen his love of nineteenth century literature. He had read *Three Men in a Boat* a dozen times, and Arsen agreed that it was one of his favorite books, too. He said he knew the Thames well. Gerald talked about Thomas Hardy, Mary Shelley, Sir Arthur Conan Doyle, Jules Verne, Nikolai Gogol, Bram Stoker, and of course, Edgar Allan Poe. "I know almost every poem he has ever written, by heart." He grew silent then, thinking about his friend the Sage, who he hadn't seen in a while.

"You miss your homeless friend," Arsen said, as if he could reach into Gerald's mind and soul.

Gerald's loneliness was spilling out. He wondered if this man next to him could smell loneliness the way he smelled the fragrances of various trees and shrubs and flowers along the riverbank. The way Gerald picked up an earthy and faint decay in Arsen's presence, and the unfamiliar cologne that almost masked the other smells.

One night Arsen asked Gerald if he had any friends. Gerald said he had many friends, the customers who came in the store, the people he worked with, people he met and talked to on the riverbank. But Gerald knew that Arsen knew the truth. He had few, if any, friends.

"I am alone most of the time, too," Arsen said.

—⁂—

Gerald didn't watch television or listen to the radio. He didn't have a computer. His source of news was his co-workers, the people he met near the river, and occasionally a newspaper. Mrs. Warstein continued to talk about the gruesome murders that held Denver in a state of fear. Police advised everyone to avoid any waterway in the Denver area at night, and the mayor ordered a curfew. Surveillance was beefed up with additional men and cameras, but it wasn't enough. The partial remains of two women had been discovered that morning.

Mrs. Warstein, still annoyed with Ted's absence, said, "Don't you hang out at that river every morning and night?" She gave him a teasing and suspicious look. Gerald nodded. She is thinking what anyone would likely think. *It's always the quiet ones.*

"You shouldn't venture anywhere near that river right now. It's too dangerous." Gerald missed the Sage and hoped he was all right.

—⁂—

Arsen didn't stop by that night, or the next. Gerald knew Arsen enjoyed rivers and creeks as much as he did. "Rivers have always been an important part of my life," Arsen had said a few nights ago. "The riverbank is where one can feel large and small at the same time, where one can be strong or fragile."

Gerald didn't understand what Arsen meant by fragile. He thought of things like fine china, crystal, glass, or plants like dandelions where the softest touch sends seeds to the wind, or newborn babies and old people. Was that what he meant?

Arsen was old. Gerald worried about him, especially with a maniac on the loose.

—⚏—

Ted's body, drained of all fluids, desiccated but intact, had been found in one of the ventilation shafts of the mall parking garage. He had been dead at least a week. Mrs. Warstein was beside herself. She relayed the news to Gerald, who also took it hard, then told him the Mall was closing early as a precaution.

Gerald thought of Arsen and asked if she had seen the old man recently. Maybe he wandered around other departments. He thought maybe he had tired of Gerald's company. Even that thought was better than thinking Arsen could have shared Ted's fate.

"What old man?" Mrs. Warstein asked.

"His name is Arsen. He's been coming in here every night just before closing, except for the past few nights. You've seen me talking to him. He even spoke to you a couple of times."

"I haven't seen any old man. I haven't seen anybody here just before closing. The store's been completely dead at that time the past two weeks, ever since those dreadful murders started happening. Oh, poor Ted..." She started to cry and wiped the tears from her eyes with her sleeve.

"Tall man, distinguished..."

She looked at him like he was crazy. "I'm not in the mood for this," she said and walked away.

She's upset about Ted, not thinking straight, he thought.

Arsen. He didn't have any idea where he lived, even what he once did for a living. He knew the geography of the man's life but hardly anything else, except he shared a love of literature and rivers.

The Sage. Now Arsen.

—⚏—

After work Gerald went home, changed into his sweat clothes, and walked to the path that led to his favorite spot along the river. It was a chilly night. He didn't see anyone out and about, not even the police, and he assumed people were simply steering clear of any place close to the river at night.

He sat on a bench between a cluster of cottonwoods. Scraggly brush and a slight muddy grade led to the river. The crescent moon was high over the treetops, dimmed by wispy clouds, and a light wind blew against the side of his face, carrying with it the fragrances of cottonwood, Indian plum, pine, and...and a whiff of cologne.

Gerald looked around. It was strangely quiet. He knew wind batted down flying insects, but there were no bird calls, no scuttling of nervous animals in the brush and trees, no sounds at all except rustling branches and leaves and the water rushing nearby.

I shouldn't be here. This is a stupid thing to do. He stood.

Something drifted across the moon. The darkness intensified as if a black net dropped over his body. The smell of cologne and decay. He knew Arsen was nearby.

And far back in his brain he knew he was going to die.

He turned away from the riverbank, and Arsen was there, not more than six feet away. Gerald gasped and dropped to one knee. It was too dark to make out any features, but he recognized the cologne and shape of shadow standing there before him, a hastily constructed puzzle of dark menace.

Before he could suck in a breath he was lifted and placed on the bench. A humming swelled into his ears, and for a long time he drowned in clouds before panic brought him back to the night and soft words. Arsen speaking to him in a slow methodical way, the way a father would speak to a three-year-old son who had just fallen off a swing.

Arsen was beside him. Gerald looked straight ahead at the river, terrified to turn and see what was next to him. Arsen stopped speaking, and they sat in silence for what seemed an eternity.

Eventually Arsen spoke again. "I knew you would be here." The water moving swiftly over rocks and against the riverbank accented Arsen's words, a white noise background. "Don't be afraid."

Gerald turned. Arsen, his features blurred and indistinct, yet larger and somehow fierce, as if some great predatory beast, the likes of which he had never seen or imagined, was viewed with a giant magnifying glass. Arsen, but not Arsen. It was not human.

The creature opened and closed its mouth, exposing jagged teeth. The eyes, mere slits, dull yellow canine eyes that stared straight ahead. It breathed in a slow rhythmic fashion, and Gerald found that his own breathing was in sync. As the creature's breathing slowed and grew calm, so did Gerald's.

"We are so fragile," Arsen said. "You and me."

"Are you going to kill me?"

"Come. The river." Arsen rose and strayed off the path into patches of weeds and knee-deep brush. Gerald followed. They stood on a shelf of rock at the water's edge listening to the soft rumbling roar of the rapids. Gerald watched the water intently, waiting for an answer.

"Edgar Allan Poe," Arsen said. Then in a gentle voice that barely rose above the sound of the rapids, he recited,

> *From childhood's hour I have not been*
> *As others were—I have not seen*
> *As others saw—I could not bring*
> *My passions from a common spring—*
> *From the same source I have not taken*
> *My sorrow—I could not awaken*
> *My heart to joy at the same tone—*

Arsen paused and looked at Gerald with a dead calm smile.

Gerald, feeling the creature's stare but keeping his eyes on the moving water, said, "'And all I lov'd—I lov'd alone.'"

The creature put its arm around him, feather light, and they stared at the water together.

"There are bigger rivers," the vampire said. "I would like you to see them."

I always wanted to write a vampire story. Shortly after moving to Denver, I went to Macy's one night to look for a new pair of shoes. The salesman was an over-the-top friendly—and likely on the spectrum—middle-aged guy who was passionate about shoes, and was an on-the-spot inspiration for the character Gerald. And it occurred to me that even monsters must get their shoes and clothing somewhere, and what if the monster took a liking to the salesperson?

The story came quickly after that. The title was borrowed from an Allen Ginsberg poem.

Tsawhawbitts Gold

Originally published in Short & Twisted Western Tales, *2020*

The shadow of a hawk passed over Del as he stood at the edge of a swiftly running creek, the bird circling several times before disappearing into the pine cover. He thought it a bad omen. Del Rourke bent and scooped a palm full of water into his mouth and face. It was brilliant cold, runoff from the peaks they had just crossed, and he wondered if there was gold there, in this spot.

Alferd ambled out of the brush after doing his business. When he saw the way Del was looking into the creek, he shook his massive painted face and snorted. "Not here," he said. "Up ahead. We follow this." He motioned toward the creek with his rifle.

Del Rourke sucked in a breath. He picked up his Winchester by the side of the creek—which he had been carrying outright since they came into this wilderness—and watched Alferd move on ahead. He was already tired of this business and was tempted to put a bullet in the back of the big man and get it over with. But Alferd knew where he was going, and he did not, even if their destination was close.

They walked their ponies beside the creek in quiet. Three pack mules followed, tethered to the ponies, all carrying supplies after two of the mules died crossing the Great Basin. It was cooler now after coming through the canyons, but Del still couldn't get over seeing the big man in front of him dressed in clown makeup. Alferd had put greasepaint on when they left Durango and kept it on the entire month they had been traveling, reapplying it when sweat and dust streaked it out.

Alferd explained it this way. Indians kept their distance from a man that looked the way he did, were respectful and afraid at the same time. Bandits and desperados thought twice about waylaying a giant man dressed as a clown this far west. And, he said, it was such an essential part of him, being a clown, that he couldn't give it up.

How the clown stumbled upon him he would never know, but when Del Rourke woke in the alleyway between the Buckshot Saloon and Mirabelle's in the little town of Durango, the first thing he saw was a blurred image of a white face with a blood-red grin staring down at him. He thought he had died. The last thing he remembered was being tossed out of the saloon into the dusty street and someone kicking him good in the side before he crawled off to sleep the bad night off. Now, something that took up his entire range of vision towered over him.

"Looks like you need a change of luck," the clown had said. There was a trace of an accent, but Del couldn't pin it down.

—⁓—

"How much further?" Del's legs ached. His head ached. The thought of gold spurred him on. "You could say something once in a while, make the journey a little more palatable."

The clown stopped. He pointed to a pictograph on a large standing rock that stood out before the towering canyon walls. There was a gathering of beads, feathers, weighted metal ornaments, tied pouches, medicine offerings. The picture on the rock was of a giant bear-like creature with a gaping jagged teeth-filled mouth, several small figures that Del assumed were braves at its feet, holding it off with spears.

It was one of many pictures on rocks and cliff walls they had passed coming through the canyons, as well as strange rock alignments and shrines where gifts such as these were piled. Alferd had pointed each one out, but this time he walked over to the picture and rubbed his hand across it. "This is recent," he said.

"I thought you said Indians don't come into these parts."

"Some warriors do, as a test, and for vision quests. Sometimes they leave an offering to the Tsawhawbitts." He turned and pulled the rein of his pony and with a subtle wave indicated that Del follow. "We are almost there."

Del was not a big man, but he was a capable one, and he knew once the huge clown showed him where the gold was, he could take care of things in a final and satisfactory way. They were as isolated as anyone could possibly be. If Del could remember his way out of the canyons, and if he could wait the winter out, he would be a rich man.

He made a mental note of the secret paths into and out of the canyons, the steep scrambles down through the occasional breaks in rimrock and a maze of lower cliffs. Tucked far in the nowhere abyss of northeast Nevada, all the gold in the world hidden right in plain sight. And it would all be his.

"Tell me about this man-eating beast," Del said.

"There's more than one of them. Lots of them. They blend in so you couldn't see one if it was five feet away." The huge clown trudged along, silent for a few minutes, as if speaking was a difficult thing. "The Shoshone legends talk about a creature thirty feet tall, but they're much smaller than that. Bigger than a man though, by a lot, and they're covered with thick reddish-brown hair. The Shoshone are right about one thing, though. They have teeth like a wolf, and I imagine they could make short work of a man."

"You've seen them?"

Alferd was quiet for a long while. The mules snorted and struggled with the heavy loads as the trail began to climb again. Then he spoke. "Saw one close up. Came around a bend in the creek, close to where we are now, and one of them was standing right in the middle of the trail. Startled the both of us. He had these sunken-in green eyes, and a flat nose, kinda like an ape. It was a male, I could tell that much, and by the look he gave me I knew it was intelligent, more like us than we'd ever want to think.

"We looked at one another for what seemed an eternity. I was so scared I couldn't move. Then it opened its mouth like it was trying to take a bite out of the air, and I saw all those sharp teeth, and I thought I was a goner. But instead of tearing into me like I expected, it dropped to all fours and disappeared into the woods without so much as disturbing a branch or a leaf."

"Maybe you saw a wolf, or a griz," Del said. "Being so scared the animal might've seemed bigger than it really was."

Alferd turned abruptly around. His mile-wide red jam mouth still in frozen smile was more menacing than ever. "You saying I'm a liar?"

"No, no," Del said, laughing to cut the tension that was suddenly in the air. His hand, though, instinctively dropped near his holster. Del's eyes stayed on Alferd's hand, which rested on the hilt of his huge skinning knife. Alferd lifted his hand and raised an exaggerated black eyebrow. "Why didn't it eat you? You're big enough to feed a whole family of those things."

"Thought about that. I was wearing my makeup, and I guess that creature never saw anything quite like that before. Maybe braves in their warpaint but not a white-faced grinning clown."

He pulled his pony along, and they continued along the creek until the narrow path turned sharply to the left through a strand of fir and whitebark pine. Within a few minutes they came upon a tiny cabin, not much bigger than an outhouse, in a small clearing of high grass and wildflowers. The ground rose sharply behind it, a snow-capped mountain blocking the western sun. Bighorn sheep grazed on the cliffs overlooking the cabin.

"Damn, looks like meat comes right to your door," Del said.

"They ain't seen much of man, so they ain't afraid."

The cabin was barely big enough for two men, but it was shelter. There was a fireplace, a table and two chairs, and one crude bunk. Two narrow windows faced out the front, remnants of greased paper flapping in one of them. After stowing their gear and eating hard tack, Alferd motioned for Del to follow him back to the creek.

They trudged through the shallow running water until they reached a bend, and Del saw a busted sluice box by the creek. "Looks like we'll be panning to start," Alferd said. "We can fix this up in a day or two."

Del nodded. "Is this the spot?"

"There's a fair amount here. A few other places."

"And you have gold hidden hereabouts?" He thought he might as well come right out and say it.

The clown stared at him.

"We're partners, right?" Del asked. "I should know in case something happens to you."

"Nothing will happen to me," Alferd said. "But, tomorrow morning, before we start to work, I'll show you one of the stashes. In good faith."

Del couldn't tell if the clown was smiling behind the obscene slash of one painted on his face.

— 〰 —

They had fresh sheep for dinner. Del popping one off the cliff just as quick darkness was falling. Del cooked his piece of meat in the fireplace, while Alferd ate his right away.

"Green," Alferd said, "the way real mountain men do it. Body warm."

The big man was not one for talking, but that night he told Del about his days performing for a small circus all over Europe. Being a clown was in his blood, and even though he walked away from it all when the circus came to the United States, he missed the life.

"Why'd you leave then?" Del asked.

The clown reached into his sack and pulled out a bottle of whiskey. After taking a long sip he passed it to Del, who also took a long sip.

"Killed a man." Alferd held up his huge hands. "Broke the son of a bitch's neck."

Del pictured the man doing that. Alferd was easily seven or eight inches taller than him, and likely close to double his weight. But even with his protruding belly, Del had seen him move with grace and ease, and the man had the stamina and strength of a plough horse.

"Why?" Del asked.

Alferd shook his head. "I don't talk about it."

Del left it where it was. He had been around long enough to know you didn't stir up a pile of dead leaves if you knew something bad was lurking beneath them. After all, everyone had things to hide this far west, or they were running from something.

Alferd never once asked anything about Del's past. Del was handy with a gun—when he wasn't drunk—and he knew he gave off an air of danger and mystery. Yet the clown-faced giant trusted him enough to make him a partner and travel hundreds of miles through isolated country without knowing anything about him. Del didn't think much about his troubled past, except in pivotal decision-making moments. Like now.

He had always been a follower. He followed Jason MacRae and about twenty other sick, starving, and scared Union soldiers who deserted during the Battle of Stones River. He followed Ike Leadfeather and his gang in Missouri and Kansas, robbing and killing settlers attempting to move west to avoid the bloodshed back east. When most of Ike's gang were hanged or killed, Del somehow managed to find work as a cowboy, following the herds of cattle from Texas to Montana. He worked when he could but always wasted his earnings on drink, gambling, and whores.

Alferd found him at one of his lowest moments and made a proposition he couldn't refuse. "I want a man who's at the bottom of the barrel but wants to climb out. I want a man with nothing to lose, who's willing to travel to the devil's lair and take from the devil himself the riches he's entitled to. I want a partner who can hold onto secrets and follow me where few men have ever gone."

So, he followed the giant clown. And he decided from the start that when the opportunity arose, he would follow no more. He would take it all from the devil.

—⚍—

A loud knock against the door woke Del up. At first, he thought it was his imagination, but a second knock came against the door with enough force to almost break the latch. Before Del could register what was happening, things crashed against the meager cabin walls from all directions, as if twenty men were hitting them with sticks and rocks. Alferd was up and at the window, shouting through the greased paper in a language Del didn't recognize.

Del grabbed the Winchester and rushed to the door, ready to open it, when Alferd yelled, "No!" The shadow form of the giant clown held his hand up, an eerie silhouette against the dull moonlit paper. A rock sailed through the paper, narrowly missing Alferd, and shattered against the opposite wall. From outside Del heard growls and barks, something scratching the wooden door, rocks crashing on the roof and rolling off.

Alferd calmly walked to his bunk, bent down, and retrieved a twin barrel scattergun. "This will scare them off." He nudged Del aside and unlatched the door. Del held his rifle ready. Through the half-open door Del saw shadows moving between the trees about twenty feet away. The growls and barks seemed to be coming from that direction, although Del thought about the cliff rising behind the cabin above them and how vulnerable the roof might be.

Alferd fired one barrel in the air, the sound echoing as if ten shots were fired. Shrieks and tongue clicks followed, then several rocks slammed into the side of the cabin. For a moment, Del thought the forests and mountains themselves were screaming, and memories of the battle he ran away from streamed into his head, the gunfire, explosions, screams, and shouts of the wounded, and the screams and shouts of the mad fighting men, a roar of blood in his ears.

And when silence came, it was like an explosion to his unraveled brain. It took several long minutes before he realized Alferd was talking to him.

"They're gone for now," Alferd said. "They knew we were here. They're an impatient lot."

"Who are they? The Shoshone?" Del walked past Alferd into the clearing. The moon was settled into a strand of pines beyond the creek. The tall grass and wildflowers were silver and wobbled in the slight breeze.

"Tsawhawbitts. Quite a few of them. They smell fresh meat."

They checked the ponies and mules who were hobbled in a nearby meadow. They were frightened but unharmed. Walking back, Del noticed large rocks and tree limbs scattered about the perimeter of the cabin. He tried to lift one of the stones but could barely budge it. "Whatever they are, if they can heft something like this, we don't have a chance."

Alferd seemed to know more than he was letting on. Del pointed his rifle at the man, the clown face shimmering in the moonlight. "What aren't you telling me?"

The clown glared at Del. He held his scattergun down, and Del knew that if there was the slightest flinch suggesting the gun was coming up, he would fire and put the clown in hell.

After a long silence Alferd shook his head slowly. "I told you they were real. They are dangerous, but they usually leave me alone." He turned away, unfazed by the rifle pointing at him. "It's good for us that the Tsawhawbitts are here. They keep everyone else away, and they could care less what we do with the gold we find. Now…if you shoot me, and I *know* that's been on your mind, you not only will never find the gold I have hidden around here, but you'll have those creatures to deal with, on your own. And if I didn't need you, I would've blown your sorry ass to the creek and beyond with the other barrel here." He laughed and went into the cabin.

—∾—

"The irony," Alferd said later that night, "is that even after quitting the business, I am still a clown. I suppose it's the same with the freaks. They are who they are, and even when they are not with the circus, they're still freaks, right?"

"How did you find this place?" Del asked. It was a long way from anywhere, and a clown, however big and proficient with knife and gun, was no real mountain man.

"The Dog Man of Leon." Alferd sipped from the bottle of whiskey. "He really wasn't from France, but he liked the exotic name. Looked like a dog, the way he was covered head to foot in fur. Somehow, he wound up finding this place, along with a friend, back before he joined up with the circus in St. Louis. He told me about it one night when he was drunk and made me a partner of sorts, thinking that I knew something about prospecting. I never let on that I didn't, and we came out here a few years back after my difficulties with the law. We did find gold. Lots of it."

"What happened to the Dog Man?" Del was getting nervous. He knew he needed to kill this man, sooner than later. The stories were not adding up.

The clown's perpetual grin widened. "Oh, he had an accident."

—∾—

The morning was cloudy gray when they started for the creek. It was eerie quiet, the birds and other animals that normally disturbed the trees and bushes and grass were silent. Alferd moved ahead with Del close behind nervously holding his rifle, jerking it left and right each time the clown stepped on a twig or kicked a pebble. Del could feel they were being watched. He tried to picture what the creatures who assaulted the cabin last night looked like. He was sure a well-placed bullet could stop one in its tracks, regardless of its size.

Alfred hadn't said a word since he had woken up. Del wasn't able to sleep, but he didn't feel tired even though it was still dark. Adrenalin coursed through his body. The nighttime visit from the creatures. The anticipation of gold. The plans that rolled around in his head. It didn't matter that the clown knew what his intentions were. Alferd was going to have his *accident* soon enough. If there was as much gold in the area as the clown let on, he didn't need to know where all the stashes were. And he had plenty of guns and ammo to stave off any threat from oversized apes.

They passed the sluice box. Followed the creek until it widened into a respectable stream, water running fast and hard, and trees on either side thick and tall. Del saw trout swimming in the ripples and shadows. A wind kicked up causing the aspens to chatter. He thought he saw movement in the pines beyond the aspens, but likely it was how the sunlight bounced around the trees, or deer hiding in the brush. He heard no sound except for the leaves and rattle of his and Alferd's pans against their packs.

Finally, Alferd said. "I'll show you some gold."

—⚌—

Alferd stopped where the stream gurgled and spat from the many protruding rocks. Del guessed the rapids were only three or four feet deep at most. The pine forest was heavy and dark on the opposite side where the two men stood, behind them a few straggling trees and a meadow with rippling grass and wildflowers of every color. The flowers were mesmerizing, and it took Del a moment to remember the plan he had come up with that morning. Once he was shown the gold, he would shoot Alferd—right here, right now—leave the body for scavenging animals. Maybe the ape creatures would drag the heavy carcass away and have a feast. No evidence.

He needed to play along with the ridiculous clown. Be grateful he was trusted with this place. Shoot the clown in the back of the head.

If these creeks were as rich in gold as Alferd maintained, he would have no trouble panning by himself. And if the hidden stash was large enough, he might just hike out of this desolate world a rich man.

"Look," Alferd said, pointing to a spot midway in the stream.

"Here?" Del didn't expect to be at the hidden place so soon. Alferd continued to point. Del stepped into the water and looked down. Though running fast, the water was crystal clear. And the creek bed sparkled as the sun reflected off hundreds of glittering specks of gold. Gold!

"Put your rifle down. Walk out to the center. It's only knee deep. This is where I hid some of the gold."

"You fool! In the open? Anybody could find it!"

"No one ever comes here. Remember, the Tsawhawbitts. Put your rifle down and look. And there's more gold than what you see here. As they say, this is only the tip of the iceberg. A golden iceberg."

Del hesitated with the Winchester. Alferd laughed. "If I wanted you dead, I would've killed you a long time ago. And why would I go to such lengths to show you where the gold is? Hold onto your rifle then. Go look."

Del nodded and smiled. The advantage was his. Looking down, stepping carefully on and around slippery rocks and sediment littered with gold specks, he moved slowly and methodically to the center of the stream where Alfred had pointed. "Where?" he said, scanning the water for any sign of something hidden away.

"Keep going. Another step or two," Alferd said.

Del looked to where Alferd stood on the bank, his legs still stepping carefully on the soft sediment beneath the rushing water.

A sharp crack, like a tree limb snapping, and immediately a searing, crushing pain in his right leg that coincided with a distant agonizing scream that he realized was his own. The rifle flew from his hands into the water and wedged between rocks downstream. The water, from where he wobbled, ran red. A bear trap, hidden in the muddy sediment, had sprung alive and bit through his leg with its massive steel teeth.

"Oh, my God!" he screamed. The trap held firm. He struggled to remain standing, the water pushing hard against him. "Help me!"

But the clown was dancing beyond the bank in the high grass, hands outstretched as if he held an invisible partner. He twirled round and round.

"Alferd! My leg is broken!" Del tried to pull the trap apart, but it was useless. Blood oozed from the leg. He sat in the rushing water on a rock, the water coming up to his stomach, the leg in the trap extended at an impossible angle. He fainted, but the cold water brought him back as soon as his face hit it, and he screamed at the clown in the meadow.

Something rushed from the woods and slapped him in the head, scratching the side of his face before disappearing into the woods again. It wasn't very large, but he recognized the burnt brown fur and the way it moved on two legs. He looked for his rifle, but it was out of reach. If there were more of those things…

Alferd stood on the bank now. His clown face seemed sad, then his shoulders heaved up and down in a pantomime act of sobbing.

"I'll kill you, you son of a bitch!" Del screamed.

The clown pantomimed shock, then exaggerated fear.

The woods on the other side of the stream came alive. One by one, the creatures that Alferd had described came out of hiding cautiously. Del realized they had likely been there all along, hidden in plain sight, watching the two men following the creek. Del figured there were maybe ten or eleven of them, of various sizes. Some huge, others small, like children. A family.

Del was thinking more clearly now, the damaged leg completely numb from both shock and the ice-cold water. He knew he had lost a lot of blood. He knew he was a dead man if Alferd didn't do something. "I should have shot you when I had the chance."

"You were greedy, though. They all were." Alferd picked something protruding from the mud by the side of the stream. He tossed it to Del. A piece of bone. It wasn't animal, like a deer or mountain lion. It was part of a man's splintered femur.

The creatures came closer but remained at a safe distance. Del turned to them, then back to Alferd, then back to the hairy monsters, all of them with mouths open, showing their teeth.

"Alferd, for the love of God." He struggled to open the jaws of the trap. "Yes. For the love of God. Or should I say, gods."

The largest of the creatures stepped into the stream. Its conical head coming right out of a massive chest. Deep-set green eyes. A skunk stench. The younger ones splashed into the water and came within a few feet of Del before stopping, cocking their heads in wonder at the fresh-caught thing in the water.

The clown spoke. "I suppose you should know. The reason I am not harmed by the Tsawhawbitts? I bring them offerings. Plain and simple. They let me have my gold, all that I want, and I give them their favorite food, which is pretty scarce in these parts. Oh, and they're afraid of clowns." He turned and began walking back the way they had come. "I don't like to watch what they do with my offerings." He patted his massive belly as he slowly walked away. "Sensitive stomach."

One of the little ones jumped toward Del and bit into his arm, tearing a piece of flesh with its sharp teeth, then splashed away before Del could even swing his other arm. Another one rushed in and took a chunk of his side. Del hit it as it moved on, but he didn't have any strength left.

"Alferd!"

The clown turned and bowed, as if he had just completed a performance. "Oh, I should tell you. They like to eat their meat green also."

It was the last thing Del heard before the creatures, all screeching and barking in a jolly mood, moved in on him.

I like western horror stories. I like clowns. I like the bigfoot legends. The Jarbidge Wilderness in Nevada gets its name from Tsawhawbitts, the Shoshone word for "a weird beastly creature." Tsawhawbitts was well known among local tribes to be a cannibalistic, man-eating giant. The Jarbidge Wilderness is one of the most remote areas in America and seemed to me to be a perfect setting for a horror western. I took creative liberties with the Tsawhawbitts legends—instead of one giant creature there are many.

The Patients In Room 116

Originally published in Sanitarium Magazine, *Issue 34, 2015*

Gloria could hear explosions in the distance. She hurried to the front entrance of Broadmore Psychiatric Hospital, her knees aching, her white uniform crinkled and wet. It was night and the building was dark. In her six-mile walk she hadn't seen a single light, a single vehicle, any sign of life. She knew there were few people left in this area, but it would have been some comfort to know she wasn't alone. She was surprised to find the doors unlocked at this hour. Anybody could get in, and the prospect of roaming through the dark with only a flashlight for a weapon wasn't something she looked forward to.

Moving as quietly as she could, she examined the main hall, the beam of light sliding across the floor and walls in steady sweeps. She checked the admitting area and the administrative offices. Everything neat and orderly and empty. The building vibrated just faintly enough to offset the pictures on the walls and raise an odor of dust. Gloria opened the door to A-Hall. She strained to hear anything, but with her hearing loss and the bombings she doubted she could hear someone or something coming after her. And she was sure that if something was hiding, she was announcing herself loud and clear with her shaking light and pounding heart.

"Anybody here?" she shouted. There was no answer. She moved on, room by room. Sweeping with the light. The nurse station was in a shambles, as if the staff abruptly left in a panic. Papers covered the floor. Overturned coffee cups, patients' charts strewn about on the desk. *They've been gone a while*, she thought. Gloria sat in one of the swivel chairs and turned the flashlight off. There were two more floors. She would check them after she rested.

This was her shift. She was responsible for D-Hall on the third floor, but the way things looked she was now responsible for the whole hospital. *Why did everyone leave? There is nowhere to go. Might as well work right up to the end. You're a good nurse,* she told herself. *You came in on schedule to care for any patients who might have been left behind. You didn't expect this.* Gloria closed her eyes. Tried to think of something else besides the throbbing of her knees. Maybe concentrate on the throbbing of her hip. Or the throbbing left-sided headache forming.

The morning started off dull red and quiet. The city, which had been evacuating steadily for days, was empty. Power everywhere was gone. Gloria was sure a few people stayed behind, but when she peeked out her window she saw nobody. Abandoned cars and trucks were cluttered about the street. Streetlights devoid of color swayed in the breeze. There was no running water, so Gloria splashed some warm bottled water on her face and armpits, put on a uniform that didn't look too bad, then sat in an oversized chair to wait for evening. She decided she would walk to the hospital when it started to get dark. She had never missed a day of work, and she wasn't going to start now.

The last news report she heard said that the jumpers were just outside the city. That's what they called them. Jumpers. She rarely listened to the news or read the papers, so, by the time the crisis was identified she was well out of the loop. People at work talked about it. She pretended to listen, but really her focus was on the patients. Jeremy said the jumpers were from another planet. Doctor Sobel said they were from another dimension, which was why the jumpers had so little substance. Beth Ann thought they were a military experiment gone out of control. Vickie just cried all the time and was of no use to anybody.

As days went by there were fewer and fewer patients and staff. Two days before, there were maybe thirty patients, most of them long-term, in the hospital, and only a handful of nurses and aides. Gloria felt like she was in a dream the past week, keeping up the routine as best she could with the patients that remained. There was enough medicine, thank God, but it was only a matter of time before that ran out.

She worked nonstop. Slept when she could at the hospital. When she collapsed yesterday morning, Jeremy drove her home, insisted she at least get a good sleep, and promised to pick her up for her shift the next day. When she noticed his belongings in the car, she knew he wasn't coming back. She hoped he made it out of the city okay. With the distant nonstop rumblings of explosions, she figured he probably didn't.

Gloria pulled herself up the stairs and opened the door to E-Hall. This was the men's floor. She stayed flat against the wall, keeping the beam of the flashlight down, edged herself slowly to where the hall ran perpendicular to another hall. Then she heard it, amidst the muffled explosions a gentle knocking, like someone calling at one of the doors. She wondered if it was a jumper, but she had no idea what they even looked like or how they behaved. It had to be a patient.

"Hello?" Quiet. Dead quiet. Even the bombings stopped. She gripped the flashlight as tight as she could. *Damn it, just walk to where the knocking came from, see what it is.* Gloria prided herself on her toughness. She had weathered the bad times just fine. Grit, that's what it was. She had grit. Put the light on Room 102. She rapped the flashlight easy on the closed door and called out again, "Hello?"

"Oh." From behind the door. She recognized the weak, grizzled voice.

"Mr. Benson, it's me, Gloria."

"How do I know it's you?"

"Who else would it be?"

"You could be one of those jumper things."

"You know my voice. Open the door."

"They can get in your head, make you believe things."

Gloria had enough. "Would a jumper jam a needle in your ass to calm you down?"

The door gave a little when she pushed on it. She pushed harder, moving the dresser that was blocking it aside. Mr. Benson, all ninety-five pounds of him, was sitting on the bed. He was wearing a nightgown and cap as if he had been lifted from the nineteenth century. His glasses were askew on his nose, gray hair puffed out from the cap.

"It *is* you," he said. He was in his upper eighties. More coherent than most of the others. Gloria was glad he was still here. She immediately checked his pulse and felt his forehead. The man was trembling, scared out of his wits.

"You're fine," she said. "Are there others here?"

"Of course. They're in their rooms. We were told to stay in our rooms. The jumpers are coming."

"Not on my watch. Come on, let's get the others. Everybody's probably scared to death." She took his feeble hand and pulled him from the bed.

He was unstable at first, but after a few minutes he was leading the way, pounding on doors and calling out names. Most of the men left on this floor were old and battling dementia. A few, like Don and Frank, were diagnosed with schizophrenia and had been in the hospital most of their lives.

There were eight men on E-Hall, and Gloria set up chairs in the hallway close to the nurse's office so she could keep an eye on them while she rummaged for their meds and some water bottles. The youngest patient, Bobby, who was in for depression, paced up and down the hall. He mumbled while the others enjoyed a cacophony of laughs, shrieks, sobs, and curses. the building shook. The bombings had resumed.

While she rummaged in the office, she wondered how it had come to this, in such a short time.

There were cracks in the sky. Black specks spewed out from those cracks like swarms of angry bees, dropping to the earth. That was the start of the war with the jumpers, the things from Mars, the dimension travelers, whatever. The places where they dropped were devastated. When the armies of the world tried to fight back, the jumpers disappeared from the engagements and reappeared somewhere else. Hence the nickname jumpers. Reports of jumpers materializing everywhere were rampant. Gloria hadn't paid much attention, of course. The patients came first.

The bombings were closer. Gloria didn't know what that meant, since trying to kill the things with conventional weapons was like swatting at flies midair. Useless. She found another flashlight that cast a dim light and gave that to Mr. Benson. She told the men to stay put while she looked for a safe place for everyone to stay. Then she planned to run upstairs to see how many women were left.

Bobby ran past her down the long hall, slammed into the door leading to the stairwell. Slammed into the door again. "I want out!" he screamed.

"We have to stay here," Gloria said, kneeling beside him, putting a hand on his shoulder. She took his hand. "Come with me."

She led him to the hall intersection, turned right, and went to Room 116, which had been unused. She unlocked the door, ushered Bobby inside, and told him to sit on one of the two beds and wait for the others. "No running off, you hear?"

He nodded meekly and sobbed. She gave him a shot of Thorazine.

The room was small, but it was centrally located. Two small dressers. Generic pictures of covered bridges in different seasons on the walls. A thick, closed-up musty smell. *This will do,* she thought.

She was in control, now. The patients needed her to be in charge, to be strong. Something was coming their way, and they had to be ready. Gloria took a deep breath. Checked her watch. 12:35.

One by one she brought the men down to Room 116. Each man was given a sedative or administered a shot. Mr. Dothers cursed under his breath.

Adam spun in circles because most of his brain was missing but was okay once he was in the room and placed in a corner. Don wanted to make love to her right then and there, because the end was coming, so why not? She declined his offer but was flattered all the same.

Room 116 was a little crowded, but the men fit nicely in it. Nobody complained.

Mr. Benson was the last one in. He asked if he could go upstairs with her to D-Hall. Gloria said no, D-Hall was off limits to men.

Before she closed the door, Mr. Benson said, "They look like dinosaurs."

"What?" she said.

"Like frogs," Don said, squeezing past the others to reach the door. "I saw pictures of them on TV the other day. You can't kill them. They can concentrate and make themselves ethereal."

"What?" she repeated.

"Like, no substance to 'em. And they can jump from one place to another in the blink of an eye."

"They won't jump here."

"What I heard."

"Stay in the room," she said. "All of you." She turned to Mr. Benson, who was holding the weak flashlight. "Don't run the batteries out of that thing. I'll be back with the women."

Don tried to angle his head out the door as she closed it. "Just bring the pretty ones," he said. "And leave Babs up there. There ain't room enough for her on this floor, let alone this room." Gloria shut the door.

Her footsteps echoed in the stairwell as she hurried up the steps. She turned the flashlight off to conserve the batteries. There was a rattling downstairs, and she knew it wasn't coming from E-Hall. She quickened her pace, one hand gliding across the railing. As she bounded to the top step her foot slid out from under her. She was down before she knew it.

Her back and neck cracked against the railing her twisted hand still clung to. Legs straight out and her butt sitting in something wet and sticky. She knew what it was. Not good. She let go of the railing and slid up to the final step. Waited a few minutes. Listened for any sound from below. Her ankle hurt like hell, but she was able to stand tentatively, steadying herself against the railing.

She groped for the flashlight. Found it resting by a sack on the landing, by the door. Only, when she turned the flashlight on, it wasn't a sack. A body, facedown, blocking the door to D-Hall. A stream of blood pooled from the neck to the steps. Five breaths. Four breaths. Three breaths. She turned the body over. The head almost flopped off, cut to the spinal cord. William. One of the maintenance guys. There were keys in his hand. Never made it to the door. If she'd had it in her to scream, she would've, but there was no time for that.

Gloria found her own keys in her uniform pocket and opened the door, pushing William aside. She pointed the beam up and down the hall. There was no activity up here, but she could detect a scraping sound that seemed to be coming from the inner walls, maybe even the stairwell on the first floor. She assumed whatever had caught poor William trying to get in the door had already moved down all the stairs. Had to be a jumper. It was a wonder she hadn't run into the thing herself.

C'mon. Don't waste time. She went to each room, knocking and opening the doors with her master key. She expected to see a dead body in every room, but each room she checked was empty. Limping from room to room. Whispering. Shaking. The back of her neck numb and stiff. The light bouncing too freely. Finally, she heard a muffled cry from room 211.

"Alma?" She broke into the room gently and efficiently. Only one of the two beds was occupied. A wrinkled ball of sheets and blankets moved slightly, and from it a withered frail little thing—drooping lips and sad sunken eyes—emerged, not at all surprised, merely obedient. Alma followed Gloria into the hall without saying a word.

In the next room they found Jennifer, another frail woman who was in an advanced stage of Alzheimer's. She was naked, and with some effort Gloria got her dressed in a nightgown. She followed Gloria, holding Alma's hand.

They found three other women on the floor. Babs, a stocky long-term patient with lips all over her face that never stopped moving. Bev, a younger depressed lady with multiple self-inflicted scars on her arms. And Mrs. Crantz, an always terrified woman, frozen silent. They found another flashlight and a few more bottles of water in the nurse's office, then moved on at a snail's pace.

The patients clung to Gloria like static balls of dust. They moved as one to the stairs, then in single file moved past William and the puddles of blood and down the steps with quiet sobs. Babs mumbled about the jumpers and the end of the world and how they were all going to die— see, look at William there.

Gloria led them to Room 116. She was relieved to hear chatter coming from the other side of the door. She knocked first and opened the door, scanning the flashlight over now hushed faces. Relief washed over every face to see her.

She directed the women into the room. "Okay, let's go. One at a time." They were hesitant. "It's all right. You'll be safe here." She pushed them in, the last patient being Alma. The patients huddled against each other.

From somewhere in the back she heard, "Bitch, give me room!"

She had given the women sedatives and hoped that that would calm everyone down some. She closed the door and locked it. Now to find some food and more water. The cafeteria was on the first floor. *Where the jumper might be.* Well. She was not one to wait for trouble to come to her. She would go to it.

Gloria had been a nurse for seemingly forever. She was tall and big-boned and had realized early on she was destined to have little social life beyond work. She didn't think she was lonely, though. The hospital had been her home for the past thirty years. The people there depended on her, and she was going to see them through this, somehow. Maybe it was a blessing she didn't pay attention to the news. Didn't have to worry about what she was up against. And thinking this, she realized the bombings had stopped again. Probably not a good sign.

She went back to the nurse's office to look for a weapon, anything she could use to protect herself. In one of the cabinets she found a steak knife and a hammer. She tied a cord around her waist for a belt and she inserted the hammer there. She decided to carry the knife.

Looking out the screened window, she could see part of the moon dipping into the trees. It was abnormally bright. Flecks of something, birds or bats, skirted across it. There were hundreds of them. If there were any sounds outside, her pounding headache overwhelmed them into silence. It was 1:37 a.m.

Taking her time going down the steps, thinking about the patients locked in Room 116, wondering if she made the right choices. They were safe for now, but would the patients have been better off scattered about like she found them? No, safety in numbers. Should she have stayed back with them? Too late, now.

Flashlight off, she felt her way, each step carefully placed. When she reached the first floor, she had the feeling she was being watched, thought about Mr. Benson's comments about jumpers getting in your head. *Non-sense. Don't let your imagination run away with you. Keep going.*

Just as she reached for the door it swung open, knocking the flashlight out of her hand. A shadow leaped into her and into the knife at the same time, rolling her and it into the wall and steps. Somehow, she kept her balance and swung her fist down onto the shadow thing, hitting something hard and wet. The thing screamed. Something metallic clattered on the floor as she scrambled to the propped open door.

"You killed me!" A man's voice. Human. Familiar.

Gloria fought hard to catch her breath. "Robert?" With her foot, she searched around for the flashlight. Found it by his shoe which held the door open. He groaned and she could tell he was squirming by the steps. With the light illuminating the stairwell she saw he was cut deep, but not serious. He was covered in blood, but she couldn't see how it had been caused by that particular wound. Another knife was several feet away. She picked it up while holding the light on his face, which was gray as his hair. Spindly arms tried to cover his eyes from the beam of light. His arms wavered like branches against the moonlight.

"They're here," he whispered. "I got one of them already."

There was dried blood on his knife handle. "You got William," she said. He shook his head. "William, the janitor."

"I saw one of them go into him," he said. "He exploded with light. He was going to kill the women up there. Ohh…it hurts."

This was too much. She started forward to check his wound but suddenly felt light-headed and stumbled backwards, all while trying to keep the light on Robert. Her eyes watering and her breaths coming in short bursts. Too fast. *Breathe slower.* She caught herself and leaned against the open door for support.

Robert was a patient on A-Hall, which was on the first floor and the first place she had checked. Robert was a sometimes delusional man, but she didn't know him to be violent. Now here he was laying on the steps covered in his blood and maybe William's blood, too. She was shaking uncontrollably. Then realized it was the building shaking.

"Oh, my God!" Robert screamed. A roar and a violent gust of wind caught Gloria and threw her into the main hall. The stairwell filled with a cloudy light rising from the floor, rising upward very fast, lifting Robert with it. The bestial roar, the likes of which Gloria had never heard before, drove nails through her eardrums and deafened her momentarily. A meaty piece of Robert slapped into the wall above her head.

There was no time to think. But she did, for what seemed an eternity. Visual scraps of her childhood flashed out of sequence, so that one moment she was a child playing with Mom, the next a middle-aged woman helping restrain a self-destructive teenager. Things became more scrambled. Being chased by teasing neighborhood children, only she was old and slow. She was a preteen girl giving a shot to a blotchy patient of indeterminate sex.

Drinking coffee and pissing in her diapers while writing in a daily log with a marvelous orange crayon. And the patients in Room 116. She abandoned them. No. She crawled, pushed forward using her legs, getting away from… whatever it was in the stairwell.

Green light spilled past her. She pushed faster then turned around, had to see what was behind her. A dim trail of green light, like slime from a slug, followed her. It showed where she had been, and, turning to look ahead where the hall went on forever, the light showed where she was going to be. Waves of the light lapped at the cafeteria entrance at the far end of the hall. Whatever had been behind her wasn't there anymore. It was dead quiet.

Using the wall to press against she slid up, surprised that the flashlight and knife were still in her hands. The hammer was still in the belt. She limped toward the cafeteria, avoiding the green light which was slowly dissipating in front of her. She caught herself groaning aloud. *Stop it. Maybe it doesn't know you're here. Maybe it left…*

Movement to her right. The light rolled up the wall like a neon shadow, then spun itself into a black hole, which quickly filled with something moving toward her, something with no real shape at first, a gelatinous wave working to change itself before it reached her. A gust of putrefied air surrounded her, everything rotten and dead she had ever smelled stinging her nostrils, trying to rip her lungs out, freezing her where she stood.

The image before her mutated into a more substantial shape. It lumbered toward her at an insanely slow speed. Gloria couldn't process the whole of what she was seeing—the human brain isn't designed for that type of trauma. Rather, she saw parts, after an initial impression of it being at once crab-like and dog-like. Four main legs driving it toward her. A multitude of small jointed legs like that of any crustacean jutting out in all directions. Dozens of fishlike eyes, some blinking, some not. A shadow-wrapped balloon body, a canine-shaped head with gnashing teeth and tentacles.

There was a clicking noise, and she realized it was her attempting to scream. She dropped the knife and flashlight. Pulled out the hammer. As it came at her, she could see the greenish light of the hellish tunnel unlocked by the jumper. She was seeing through the thing. There was nowhere to go. But she moved anyway.

Gloria lunged and swung the hammer with all her might. Swung right through the jumper, which stopped and reared, roaring as it came down on her. She never broke the movement, spinning around with the hammer as if caught in a cloud whirlpool. This time the hammer connected with something. The jumper shattered like glass, showering the hallway with thousands of crystalline beads that popped and fizzed before disappearing into the floor.

The tunnel and green light evaporated. Every cell in her body trying to take in an agonizing breath, she stared at the empty spaces of dark which never looked so wonderful. "Guess you lost your concentration," she mumbled.

The cafeteria had been ransacked, but Gloria still managed to find a handful of granola bars and some overripe bananas. As she was leaving, a thought occurred to her. If William had stayed behind, maybe he'd had a plan of action, maybe there was another reason he was going up to the patients. Maybe he wasn't the monster Robert said he was.

She hobbled to the maintenance administrative office, which was across from A-Hall. The door was open. Piled on one of the desks was an assortment of tools, including a crowbar, machete, and several flashlights. She started to cry as she scooped everything she could into a daypack that was lying on the floor. Holding the crowbar in one hand and putting the machete in the cord about her waist, she hefted the daypack over her shoulder. She winced but was feeling better about everything.

"Don't know what you were planning, William," she said aloud, "But thanks."

The only sound was the wind whistling through the cracks beneath the windows at the far end of the hall. Her watch still worked. It was 3:12. This was the quiet time. When she worked this shift, she was usually writing in the log or cleaning the office. Most of the staff dozed off. The foggy hours, Gloria called this time. She never napped on duty.

It took forever to make her way to the stairs. She was exhausted. Close to being completely broken. Every cell in her body disobedient. Even her brain struggled with colliding thoughts and impressions. Was there more than one jumper in the building? Did she really kill it, or was that an illusion? What was happening in the outside world?

"Damn it, stop thinking," she said. *Concentrate on the here and now, the immediate goal. Get this stuff to the patients. Make sure they're all right. Do your job. Hoping the army will come to the rescue won't do any good. Worrying about what might be behind each door...*

It was the screech that jerked her head around and down, ducking just in time as splinters of wall exploded in all directions, blinding her for a moment and smashing her leg in a torrent of pain. The pack slid across the floor, which was tilting at an impossible angle, as if something pushed it from underneath. She followed the daypack toward a cloud with teeth, tentacles reaching out and wrestling with her damaged leg.

This is it. I'm going to die. It had come through the wall, or the floor, must have smelled or tasted her presence, and there was enough substance to it to finish what the other jumper had started.

She pulled the machete from her belt as she slid. Struck at the thing, but it was like swiping at thin air. Her kicks sometimes went through the tentacles, sometimes not, as the substance of the jumper faded in and out. It was real enough, often enough, to wrap around her legs and pull her towards something resembling a black hole with canine teeth. She jabbed with the machete. The teeth clamped down on her kicking legs but lost substance; instantly her legs were numb, somewhere else, then feeling came back as the jumper reopened its mouth to bite again.

She threw herself forward, machete connecting with the inside of the black hole mouth, solid now, real. Vomit spewed out from the thing, engulfing her in blood, bile, flecks of bone, burning her skin. She rolled to the side, or was thrown to the side, and was free of the tentacles. Slid in the vomity muck along the side of the wall. Covered her head to try to shield herself from the next onslaught. Music, the vocals in a foreign tongue, played from the walls, the ceiling, the floor, decreasing in volume until fading out completely.

She had to look. The jumper was gone.

Gloria grabbed the machete. With the crowbar she propped herself up. Bolts of pain shot from her ankle up her leg into her lower back, but with the crowbar she could move Quasimodo-like. She found the daypack and then the stairs and moved on, the stench of the creature's vomit and the pain in her leg numbing her brain.

She crawled up the stairs to the second level. Inched her way along the wall to Room 116. Opened the door. They were all asleep, every one of them, on the floor and in the beds, the sedatives she had given them effective. She quietly checked each patient, then went back into the hallway, gently closing the door.

A screeching roar. She saw the jumper, bathed in light, skittering on crustacean legs at the end of the hall by the dayroom. This one had no defined head. Nothing that resembled eyes. It was like a glass ornament from hell with fluid knobs and tentacle-like appendages twisted about each other. A swirling hole widened in its center like a whirlpool. The jumper stopped moving.

Gloria was beaten. There was nothing left in her. So, she was surprised when her legs, with the help of the crowbar, moved toward it. The closer she got, the smaller it looked. Its jointed legs scratched into the linoleum floor and the plaster walls, tentacles flapping and waving like flames. Gloria focused on the pulsating hole, assuming it had to be the mouth, the weakest point.

It was waiting for her. It had to be intelligent, but she sensed pure malevolence, something that saw her as nothing more than an annoying speck in its way. As were all humans, apparently. She didn't give a shit. This was here and now. She was going to defend her nest.

The jumper roared again. The blast of its breath almost knocked her down. The hole swirled and closed. Opened again. Gloria heard a crackle of static. Out from the hole came a scratchy version of "The House of the Rising Sun," as if the thing had channeled into a faraway radio station.

Gloria threw herself into it. "I." *Thwok.* "Like." *Thwok.* "That." *Thwok.* "Song." *Thwok. Thwok.*

The sound of breaking glass A shrill hiss of escaping steam and sounds she couldn't register with her earthly experience. The beast shattered into thousands of sparks. A thousand hail stones. A thousand drops of nothing. Then darkness.

The building was quiet. In the distance the bombings had resumed. Maybe they had never stopped. Did it matter? Gloria stretched, every muscle crying in pain. Yes, she decided, it did matter.

Her shift would be over soon. No doubt she would have to work a double. She went into the office and sat at the desk. Found the logbook and a pen. Pulled out a pair of bent reading glasses. She wrote: "All the patients in Room 116 sleeping peacefully." Then she closed her eyes.

"The Patients in Room 116" was one of the earlier stories I wrote, although the first version was more of a psychological horror story and much shorter. I submitted the story to Charles L. Grant for his Shadow *series in the early eighties. He sent me what is probably the nicest rejection letter I've ever received, written in longhand, almost apologizing for not accepting it. Bottom line was that it was too short, and he didn't understand the story, which, he explained, was his problem, not mine.*

I filed the story and forgot about it for a little over thirty years. Then I dug it out, put in some science fiction elements, lengthened it by a lot, and sent it to Sanitarium Magazine. *I didn't hear back from them, and after a year, assuming it was a lost cause, I started submitting it elsewhere. No responses.*

Then, months later, out of the blue, I received an email from the editor of Sanitarium, *Barry Skelhorn, apologizing for the delay, and that if I agreed they would love to publish the story. It apparently had been lost in the slush pile.*

Accidental Absence

Originally published in The Horror Zine *Fall Magazine, 2019*

Jake Olmstead closed his dry cleaning shop early in the evening, feeling feverish and weak. Most of the shops and businesses on Main Street were already closed and dark, and there was no one about at all.

A cold wind met him as he walked towards his house a quarter-mile away, the yellow moon not quite full, indigo clouds cutting across it like slivers of dark glass. He thought it unusual that things were so empty and desolate looking, as if he was the last person on earth. His heartbeat raced, and his bones ached to the marrow. Perhaps everyone in the little town of Mount Healthy had already succumbed to an outbreak of influenza.

Emma would be at her book club meeting, which met every other Wednesday night, and wouldn't be home till late. He was going to have to fend for himself.

Trees shuddered and leaves skittered across the sidewalks as he walked, the wind in his face. He passed the woods on his right, no houses for a good stretch, and with the night coming down hard Jake had to strain to see where he was going. In his weakened condition the last thing he needed was to trip and fall over a dead branch or an uneven crack.

The woods. The woods defined the town, surrounded it and cut it off from the rest of the world. The woods held many secrets. He thought, as he always did when he walked home alone at night, of William, his once-best friend.

"Sleep well," he said, looking into the dense shadows of the silent woods. He shuddered. "Sleep well."

The house was completely dark when he finally made it to the front steps. Leaves were brushed up in a pile against the front door. His nose had started to run, and his head already felt clogged up, but Jake was still able to smell something dead in the air. *Must be something big*, he thought, *if I can smell anything*. He had caught a whiff of it as soon as he turned up his walkway and entered the yard. It became stronger the closer he came to the house, and now at the door it was almost overpowering. *Get inside quick.*

He unlocked the door, thinking back to the time years ago when one didn't need to lock doors, everything safe then. No, that was wrong. It was never safe. Crazy, fucked up world. What had happened to William was proof of that. Accidents happen. And sometimes accidents fix things. But not all the way. He knew Emma thought about William all the time even though she never mentioned his name anymore. That was something Jake could never fix.

He was deteriorating fast. All that was on his mind now was taking his temperature and getting in bed. No need to call Emma. She wouldn't be home for at least a few hours, and there was really nothing she could do for him anyway. He just needed sleep.

Jake entered the house and closed the door quick behind him, hoping none of the noxious smell followed him in. He flipped the front hallway light switch. Nothing. He was a little dizzy. He felt his way to the kitchen, flipped that light switch. A dull, uneven light came on, just enough to bring out the shadows. He went straight to the kitchen sink, found a glass in the cabinet above, filled it with water, and took a gulp.

He spat it out immediately. "Damn!" *What the hell?* It tasted like sewer water. He held the glass up to his watery eyes. In the dismal light it appeared normal. He dumped it out, refilled it again after letting the water run awhile. He held onto the sink for support, his weakness getting the best of him.

He smelled the water before putting the glass gingerly to his lips. Water tasted like shit. Like something had crawled into the pipes and died there.

He put the glass in the sink. Well, he would have to deal with this issue tomorrow. Call a plumber and get him out here first thing to look at it. Right now, he needed to just get in bed.

"Simpson!" he called out. Where was that cat? He noticed the bowls on the floor, one filled with cat chow, untouched. Odd. Simpson ate anything, anytime, which was why he was so fucking fat, and he always crept out from wherever cats hide to see who came home. Even fat lazy cats are curious. Maybe he was upstairs. Or in the basement.

The basement door was closed. Of course! The door somehow closed on the poor guy, trapping him down there. Jake opened the door and called Simpson a few times. He didn't have the strength or desire to go down the steps to look. His head was humming, his ears were now plugged from the congestion. He left the door open and decided to go upstairs. Cats do what they want to do.

The house was so dark. The kitchen light did almost nothing. Why didn't Emma leave any lights on when she left? Jake tried another hallway switch. That one didn't work either. Probably burnt out like the other one. *Well, lived in this old house for over thirty years, ought to be able to find my way to the bedroom.*

He was still dizzy and scolded himself for not getting something to drink from the fridge. It took forever to make his way up the stairs, which, once he did, the walls and ceiling of the upstairs hall, barely discernible, seemed impossibly long and forbidding.

Jake took slow, unsteady steps. Things appeared darker than they should have, as if whatever light escaped from downstairs was bottled up and placed out of reach. He couldn't ever remember being this tired and thirsty. It made his brain fuzzy. He sensed the blackness in the hall matching the blackness growing inside his skull.

He felt along the wall, his trembling hand sliding across the cool plaster. *Should find the door opening soon. Where the hell is it?*

Next thing, he was stumbling. Tripped over something on the floor, something soft, and with both hands flailing he went down. Not hard. He was able to break the fall somewhat, but he felt his knee twist, same knee that always gave him trouble, a tearing pain stabbing him there. He groaned and pushed against the wall.

"What the hell?" he mumbled, now rubbing his knee, feeling a single extra-large needle jab just beneath the kneecap, then numbness radiating out from that spot. "Really did it this time." A flash of pain deflected the next thought for a moment. *What did I trip over?*

He groped about. Reached toward the center of the hallway. The pain excruciating as he moved. His hand settled into a puddle of wet fur.

Jake screamed.

Panting. *Collect yourself.* Felt around the mass, fur, wet and mushy, like a soggy stuffed animal. About the size of…

"Simpson?" He nudged the unmoving thing, tried to lift part of it off the floor, shifting his own body to get a little leverage, but the throbbing in his knee and the dizziness kept him from doing so. He didn't think he could get up. Crawl to the bedroom and turn the light on. Surely *that* light had to work. Damn.

Using his arms, he dragged himself toward where he thought the bedroom should be, pushing with his good leg wherever he could get traction. The wood floors were wax slick, and it seemed to take forever. He was totally out of breath by the time he reached an empty space along the wall and could feel the door frame.

"Jesus," he said, slowly squeezing into the room. He pushed up with his leg, pressed his body into the frame, then tried to grip enough of the wood to pull himself into a somewhat erect position. As he did so he swung his right arm out trying to find the light switch. Nothing. Damn it all. He swallowed, tasted bile, and slid to the floor again.

There was a noise downstairs.

Jake's first thought was that it was Emma, and he almost called out. But something wasn't right. He stopped moving and listened. Something *was* downstairs. Something dragging itself across the linoleum. He thought he heard the slightest moan almost drowned out by a soft thump and creak of the floorboards, as if whatever was moving was shifting its heavy weight around in the kitchen.

Come on, he thought. *I'm delirious, hearing things.* He put his hands to his ears and felt the sticky wetness from the thing in the hall, then wiped them on his trousers. Closed his eyes tight to make it all go away.

Maybe it *was* Emma. Home early. And, since the lights weren't on, thought he wasn't there. Jake took a few deep breaths, then called out, "Emma? That you?"

Silence. Whatever had been moving around down there stopped.

He was breathing rapidly. His legs pins and needles. Arms weak. *Am I having a heart attack?* He tried to call out again, but all that spilled from his mouth was a groan. The dragging downstairs started again. Then a thump, thump, thump, growing fainter as if a sack of potatoes had been dropped down the basement steps. Panic mixed with fever delirium took over, and he pushed his frail body tight against the wall. He waited. The voice in his head that urged him to remain calm and think rationally was now screaming and saying things in languages he had never heard before.

He pounded on the floor. The screaming in his head stopped. His calm voice was back. Intruders. Had to be. They had already been upstairs and killed Simpson, why, he couldn't fathom. Now they were downstairs looting the house.

Why was he thinking it was more than just one intruder? Didn't make sense, but he felt it, and he had to go with that. He must've surprised them when he came in, and again fear swept over his thoughts. Why were they still here if they knew he was here, too? If they were capable of killing Simpson, then…

He had to do something. Find the phone. Call for help.

On his elbows, and drawing his good knee in, he managed to crawl to the nightstand by the bed. He pulled the phone off and down to the floor. No ringtone. Dead.

Now anger replaced the panic and fear. He crawled to the doorway. Adrenalin overpowering whatever illness had been crippling him earlier. He might go down, but by God he would go down fighting. He had served in Vietnam. Saw a fair amount of action, maybe even killed a man. There. He was never sure. But, no matter. Whoever was downstairs was in for a fight.

Gathering as much spit in his mouth as he could, he bellowed out, "Hey!" He pounded the wood floor again with his fist. The pounding echoed in his head like the sonar ping inside a submarine. He thought he heard a whooshing sound as if air was being squeezed out of a balloon.

Steps. Slow. Methodical. Heavy on the wood floor downstairs, muffled when crossing the area rugs. The footsteps stopped at the bottom of the steps. By the sound of it, there was only one person down there. Jake stayed completely still. His breathing clipped rasps. A pain in his chest eclipsed the needle pains in his knee. He had to move. If he was going to die, he wanted to be moving, not cowering in the doorway.

Jake pulled himself forward into the hall, crawled the best he could, panting, heart racing.

He made it past the muddled remains of what he assumed was Simpson. Hands slipping in wet goo as he passed. The smell of death and decay greeted him as he reached the landing.

Whoever it was waited at the bottom of the steps, silent. Jake felt a presence there, and somehow it seemed a familiar presence. He took hold of the railing and pulled himself up, tottering, not sure he could put any weight on his leg to move downward. To engage whoever awaited him. He stopped and caught his breath. Even with his heart out of control, spasms of pain, and a useless leg, he was ready for battle.

"What do you want? I have a gun," he lied, knowing deep down it was a useless threat. Jake listened hard for a response, a movement, a breath from the presence at the bottom of the steps, one he couldn't see but sensed. Nothing.

Emma came to his mind. He was glad she wasn't here but thought of the anguish and pain it would bring if things didn't go well, and how she might react finding him the way he found Simpson. Would she miss him as much as she secretly missed William? Jake squeezed his eyes shut. Where did that thought come from? Damn him! About to fight for his life and the man was creeping in his thoughts out of nowhere.

He wanted to say to Emma, so many times, that the man she loved and missed so much never went far away, was just in those woods over there. Someday you can visit him. We'll go together…

Now there was someone at the bottom of the stairs, in the dark, waiting, motionless. The death stench was overpowering. Jake was at the top landing, an advantage, although he had no idea if the intruder had a weapon. *He must have one, to still be here.* Jake had nothing. The feeble kitchen light was out. The darkness was an ally for both of them, but his eyes were old and slower to adjust. If the man came running up the steps, Jake might have a chance to throw him off balance.

Like he had with William, so long ago.

He remembered standing over the twisted body of his friend, and Simpson, somehow there in the middle of it all, jumping off the second or third step and landing on William's contorted face. William was dead.

It was an accident. But it became something else. Jake buried William in a remote part of the woods. He took William's car, drove to his house, packed several suitcases, put them in the car, then submerged the car in a deep part of Cooper's Lake. Everyone would think William left town suddenly. He walked home past the woods where William rested for all eternity and got back before Emma, who had been at her book club meeting.

She was heartbroken that her lover left her, even though she never showed it. He was not going to let her heart get broken again.

As his eyes slowly adjusted to the shifting grays and blacks within the house, he made out a silhouette below the stairs, motionless, but larger than he expected. A sliver of light crept in behind it, what little moon there was slipping out of the clouds into the decorative glass on the front door. The faintest amount of light drifting through the shadow form of the intruder as if it had no more substance than a dissipating cloud.

"Go away," Jake said. "Just go away."

The form below him seemed to nod its head. Jake could see fine strands of what appeared to be hair, silver in the minimal light, threading upward with static excitement on an invisible breeze. It was familiar. Waiting. Wanting. Needing.

"Jake."

He recognized the voice. He took a step back, but his foot hit something, something that had not been there before, something moving enough to throw him off balance.

Oh my God oh my God oh my God. Jake went sideways, scratching at the air to catch hold of anything to stop the momentum taking him down, down to that thing, that abomination standing in the darkness waiting for him, somersaulting and crashing all the way, the steps deep and forever long. There was snapping like brittle twigs crushed underfoot, and the emotions of terror, love, guilt, and surprise melding into one before everything went completely black.

—⚍—

Emma Olmstead approached the house at ten thirty. Her good friend, Mary, had just dropped her off and was waiting in her car for Emma to get safely inside. Emma thought for sure she had left the outside light on, as well as the hallway light, but the house was completely dark.

Emma unlocked the door and waved Mary off. She waited for a second until Mary's headlights disappeared along with the fading hum of the Buick's engine, the only sound remaining the scratch and skitter of fallen leaves and the groan of tree branches against the wind.

She wasn't used to being out this late. She noticed the sliver of moon across the street, rising above the gnarled trees. So peaceful, she thought. So lonely.

This was always the hardest part, coming home at night, opening the door, flipping on the hallway light. The first thing she would see would be the bottom of the stairs. Where she discovered the broken body of Jake so long ago, along with Simpson. He had apparently tripped over the cat and fallen down the steps. Both were dead. Sometimes, in the instantaneous eruption of light, she saw a flash of him crumpled before her, the way unscrupulous film editors used to splice an image of popcorn or a burger to plant hunger in unsuspecting filmgoers. She could never lose the thought that he was always there, still, waiting to be discovered.

She stared at the stairs a long moment, longer than usual, thinking of Jake, then William, out there somewhere. She was sure he would someday come back, would come to this house to take her away with him. And, as she did every night, she turned the outside light on so that William would know someone was home. She left the light on all night, every night.

It was why she'd never left this awful place. She couldn't bear the thought of William coming back and her not being here.

Emma sighed. So many years alone in an old house with nothing but bad memories. She slowly crept into the kitchen and poured herself a glass of water before going to bed.

"Accidental Absence" was inspired by a chapter in an unfinished novel of mine, a novel I've been playing with for many years. I took the main idea of the chapter, that of a ghost caught in a loop, constantly reliving his last hours of life, and wrote my first ghost story. The original version depicted Jake's abused and deceased daughter as the ghost, but when I submitted the story to Jeani Rector at The Horror Zine, she felt a little girl wasn't menacing enough. I changed the ghost to be a friend of Jake's who had been having an affair with his wife.

A Touch Of Shade

Originally published in Broadswords and Blasters, *Issue 11, 2019*

Darling crawled the last fifty yards to a ravine that shimmered and danced in the white-hot sun like a deep pool of water. His arms were almost useless now, blackened appendages, blistered and raw, encrusted with blood and other burning fluids leaking out. His lips were swollen and seemed to be growing over his face like a grotesque mask. It felt that way. They were likely gone.

Whatever was left of his mouth barely allowed little sips of air to squeeze through. His brain stopped moving a long time ago, but his body didn't know it was dead. It moved on. Everything was too bright, the sun resting on his back and shoulders pushing him into the molten hot earth that shoved back at him in protest. He saw only blinding white. He wanted shade. He needed shade. Without it, he knew he would die.

The sun was high above, mid-day, and he saw through torn squinted eyes there was no shade here. He almost laughed. No brush high enough to offer any kind of relief from Hell. Sagebrush and mesquite, and rocks, lots of rocks, no bigger than his fist. He would give anything for a touch of shade.

―⁂―

Three days earlier he and his compadres surprised a small band of Apache, killing all of them. It didn't matter that they were all starving old men, women, and children. They took scalps not because of any bounty but because they liked it. Once, they made a considerable fortune providing scalps to the governor of Chihuahua, no matter that they were often Mexican scalps instead of Apache, Comanche, or Navajo. Now there was a price for their scalps as well from that same governor if they dared venture that far south.

The six of them rode northwest. Constant, their leader, a burly, hairy man who resembled some kind of demon with his stovepipe hat adorned with feathers and his saddle with scalps—out front with his black stallion. And the others—Badger, Crying Tom, Riley, Carlos, and himself—sauntering along like they had all the time in the world to get nowhere. They left the scalped and mutilated bodies for the coyotes and vultures.

"Savages got what they deserved," Constant said, spitting a piece of flesh from his mouth the way he would a chaw of tobacco. The little girl the flesh came from gave him more of a fight than he expected, and her scattered body parts attested to that fact.

Darling wiped a bloody hand across his filthy forehead and laughed. "Practice, boys, practice!"

They headed toward the foothills of the Gila Mountains, bloodlust in their eyes and a hunger for the wealth of lone prospectors and the occasional misdirected wagon bound for California. He thought about the shriveled white-haired old man who spat curses at them as they flayed him alive. Carlos, half Indian himself, was thoroughly spooked and muttered prayer after prayer.

"Come on," Darling said. "He's no different than any other savage we kilt the past two years, 'cept maybe a little less fight in him."

"I recognized some of those curses," Carlos said. "And I remember the look in his eyes even after he was dead. He was no ordinary old man. He said he will come for us as Chunuxu, Scalped Man, only he will borrow the body of Owl Man."

Darling and Riley, riding nearby, laughed.

Darling said, "I can shoot the feathers off any flying demon, any time."

Carlos didn't say anything but stared straight ahead as if continuing prayers in his head.

The heat was upon them as they rode on, slow and deliberate. Darling saw the outline of mountains directly ahead and was thankful they had several mules laden with supplies and plenty of water. "He weren't no different than any burnt savage we trimmed," he said to Carlos. "No offense, my friend." His right hand resting on one of the three revolvers on his person and his eyes steel-cold, serious.

"He was a magician," Carlos said. Then thinking of the companions around him, said "But he bled no different than any other dog, that is true."

They camped in a tight canyon that night, one that yielded no water and little relief from the sun during daylight. Carlos scouted for any sign of Apache and was satisfied that even the creatures from Hell itself needed a break from this kind of desolation.

The men were well armed and vigilant. Constant was determined to be in the mountains within a few days, and nothing on this earth was going to stop him from the plunder that awaited him. He marched around the perimeter of the camp on the first watch, dazzled by the millions of pinprick sparkles in the sky. Darling watched his shadow-form move in and out of his range of vision, laying on his side trying to ignore Badger and Crying Tom's air-ripping snoring. Hell, any Apache in a hundred miles would awaken to that and come at them with a vengeance, but Constant didn't mind. To him, their little band of mercenary scalp hunters was invincible.

Darling didn't see the point of going much further with this bunch. He was tired. He had enough money from the unlucky immigrants who'd stumbled their way a week before. At first the three humble wagons containing two families were frightened to see the six men coming at them dressed in their best hellish garb of human skin masks and bloody top knots stringing along like unholy banners. The men of the party they approached stood with rifles ready but let them dip down when they saw they weren't Indians.

By the time they realized how heavily armed Constant's men were, it was too late. The six men were armed better than some armies, with two or three pistols apiece, rifles, tomahawks, and genuine Bowie knives. Constant came at a full gallop after giving the immigrants a rousing hello and dropped the largest of the men with his swivel-bore rifle. He dropped the man next to him with the same rifle almost as fast, and the rest of the outlaws swooped in and dispatched the third man with multiple shots from their pistols.

They killed all of them, fourteen men, women, and children. They took whatever they could find of value, loaded the bodies in the wagons then burned them. Darling, for the first time in his life, found the killings distasteful. He had always found killing to be an essential skill in the wilderness, even enjoyed killing when the blood was up. He was good at it, and it was natural to fall in with men of similar like. They rode slowly away from the burning carnage as they always did after a raid, heading west toward the mountains and the promise of more wealth. Darling decided he would do no more killing. He had enough money to strike off on his own once they made it to the mountains, settle somewhere in California.

Then they found the small band of Apache. He realized he was what he was, an animal that could no more give up killing than not take a breath of air.

Darling thought of the old man Carlos called a wizard. No, a magician. He died easily enough. What is dead, is dead. The old man may have had some powerful magic, but it didn't do him any good in this life, and he doubted it would do him any good in the great beyond.

No way he was going to sleep with the noises the animals were making around him. Between the snoring and the farts and the incessant rustling Darling expected he would be up until his watch unless he shot the sons of bitches for the quiet. He watched a shooting star disappear into a cloud. A cloud that seemed to be swallowing stars as it dropped. As Darling started to rise, a shrill scream split his ears. Then Darling was on his feet running toward what he thought was Constant, a shadow among many shadows descending, not more than twenty yards from the smoldering campfire.

It was Constant screaming. The scream of a man being skinned alive, burnt, or ripped apart by animals. Darling had both his pistols out and didn't wait before firing at the shadows that seemed to be hovering over what was left of Constant. There was no thought in this, it was reflex, and he charged at the shapes, screaming himself, firing blindly, emptying the chambers by the time he was upon the slaughtered mess that was once their leader. More shots rang out as the others, cursing and shouted, stumbled around Darling.

The shadows were gone. Spots of stars again disappeared as whatever attacked the camp and ravaged Constant went back toward the heavens.

"What the hell?" Badger fired his Colt Dragoon into the disappearing holes in the sky. Riley and Crying Tom ran to Constant, now spread out in pieces about the camp. Something fell on Carlos who lingered back by the remains of the campfire.

"Ch'iidii!" The object that had fallen on his shoulder fell into the ashes, and when he saw it resembled a human hand with the fingertips chewed off, he dropped to his knees and began chanting, "Hiyiyiyiyi, Hiyiyiyiyi…"

Riley picked up Constant's head by the hair and looked into the eyeless pits. "Damn Constant. You was the most foul thing on this earth but din't deserve this." Still dangling Constant's bloody head, he turned his attention to Carlos. "What's he doin'?"

"Apache death chant," Darling said. His heart raced and he was as alert as he had ever been in his life.

Carlos stopped chanting and an eerie silence ensued where every man

keened their senses to the world around them, waiting for whatever attacked their leader to come back and finish them off.

"What done sneaked up on him?" Badger asked. The giant man resembled a bear more than anything human, got the name Badger for biting
off a chunk of a black bear's nose once. He was a tenacious fighter, if slow
witted, and Darling was thankful he was with the man, not against him.

"Weren't no Indians, that's for sure." Darling strained his eyes to see
anything in the desert wilderness, the stars giving little light and the moon
barely a sliver. "It looked like birds what got him, the way they flew off."
He shivered in the cold night air.

"No birds done this," Riley said. He started gathering his bedroll and
saddle. "I ain't for sticking around."

"The old man's magic," Carlos said, also gathering his things. "Those
scalps of ours, the owners are coming back for them." He tore the tangle
of scalps that adorned his saddle and tossed the bloodied clutter to the
ground, then kicked ash and dust over them.

"That's money you're throwing away," Darling said. "I don't believe in
monsters or angry spirits. This was real."

"The spirit world is real," Carlos said. "We sent enough topless souls
there. I think that makes it so."

"Let's pack up then, get going." Darling sized up his remaining companions. He tolerated them the same way they tolerated him. None of
them was a man he could call a friend, none of them a man he could truly
trust. Each of them would just as soon slit your throat as shake your hand,
yet they needed each other in their enterprises of late. Maybe Carlos was
right. They were a demon lot to be sure, and perhaps there was something
out there, exacting revenge. Best they get on to the mountains and away
from here.

They rode through the rest of the night. The lightening dawn scratched
at their backs and threw shadows before them as the morning progressed.
Normally, Darling enjoyed watching the sun rise out from the horizon, a
rare treat since they often traveled before the first light. Now he nervously
kept glancing back to make sure nothing was following them or dropping
from the pink sky.

The terrain was mercilessly flat and harsh with small rocks and saguaro,
cholla, and other cacti. The ponies struggled. Already the heat was rising.
There was no shade, no place to stop and rest from the unrelenting sun.
They decided to walk the ponies.

"Mountains are further away than ever," Riley said, his striped tattooed face hidden beneath his wide brimmed hat. "I've never been on this stretch before, that I can remember."

"Looks like a large rock up ahead, might give some shade. We can rest there," Darling said.

Carlos remounted and headed for it. He was always point man. The rest walked single file with their ponies and the pack mules. Badger struggled in the rear, falling further and further behind. When Darling turned to urge him on, he saw dark specks in the sky approaching Badger from behind, growing larger by the second.

"Look at that," Riley said. The specks were coming on, swirling far overhead Badger, who was having a hard time of it, oblivious. "Looks like buzzards. Jesus." He realized they were anything but.

"Badger!" Darling called out. But it was already too late. The specks became discernable figures by the time they swirled down to the big man, and the shock of what Darling and the others saw delayed their reaction times in drawing their weapons. The monsters that descended on Badger before he even turned around were the size of large humans but had the feathered shape of owls, with wings and talons. Their heads were hybrids of humans and birds with sharp curved beaks protruding from skull-like faces. Strands of hair from the tops of the skulls streamed behind like confetti, as if they had been scalped in a previous life.

Two of the creatures dug into Badger with their talons and lifted him off the ground. A third flew into him beak first and penetrated deep in his abdomen, while Badger frantically yelled and struggled to free himself. He struck one of the bird-like creatures but was already hundreds of feet high in the air, his legs wiggling and kicking as if he was being hung by a rope.

A shrill cry came from the creatures as they proceeded to tear him apart and feed. There were more of the monsters than Darling could count, and a wave of darkness came at the remaining men standing their ground, almost hypnotized by the unbelievable sight coming at them.

Darling fired first, hitting one of the owl creatures in the chest. The creature wobbled in the air and dropped to the ground, not dead but disoriented for a second. It continued toward Darling on foot. He shot it two more times then took a bead on another beast that came over his head, going for Riley who was firing his pistols in every direction. Darling fired and the creature's head jerked into a spray of blood and yellow pus. It dropped to the ground, too, spinning in circles but still moving toward Riley.

A multitude of cracks came from Riley and Crying Tom, who were well behind him now heading for the ponies. Darling swung his empty pistol and struck a wing moving past him at incredible speed, the force knocking him into the hard earth. The ponies screamed. All sense left him as he scrambled on the ground with his empty pistol still in hand, trying to find his way in the swirling dust and blood to the others still fighting.

He saw Carlos way off by a big rock, watching, then speeding away on his pony. Suddenly the pony's legs were gone as if a giant scythe swept through them. A black cloud fell on Carlos before he could rise from the ground.

Riley and Crying Tom knelt by the downed ponies as the winged creatures dove and slashed with their talons and beaks. Darling was almost there. Crying Tom screamed at the top of his lungs in fury as he blasted at the beasts with Constant's swivel-bore.

Then Darling was in the air, talons dug deep in his leg. His pistol dropped. The creature's massive wings carried him high and away from the carnage below. The pain like multiple knives thrust into him. He dangled upside down, saw a brief image of what appeared to be hundreds of shadows swarming and enveloping the remains of his companions.

He reached to work at undoing the claws from his leg then pulled his Bowie from its sheath. As the creature turned its head to look at him, Darling stabbed upward into its chest. He got a clear look at the skull-like face with the curved beak, almost human for a moment, then the rank rotting smell from its mouth when it screeched in pain overwhelmed him, and he blacked out.

Darling came to on the ground. He knew immediately his legs were broken and useless. Shots coming from far away, then the cacophony of screeches and high-pitched wailing beyond the desert slope. He pulled himself to a good-sized boulder and waited while the sun blistered and blackened his skin.

It wasn't long before it was dead quiet. Darling struggled to a leaning position against the rock, squinted to see around him and saw nothing but a wavering mix of blue and brown, sometimes a brief slice of the great empty plain he was in, stretching out in an arc, with the mountains more distant than ever behind him.

To stay put in this heat was to die. He checked his injuries. By the swelling and pain, the right ankle was broken but he could move the leg enough to use his knee to help crawl. The left leg felt as though it was filled with fire ants and scorpions and dangled out at an angle like a scarecrow's trousers filled with straw. He covered his hatless head the best he could by pulling up his jacket. He sucked up the pain, remembering the times he had been shot or stabbed and survived just fine. He crawled toward the mountains.

It was slow. He stopped every few minutes to scream in agony. The white sun crushing. If he didn't find shade or water, he would die. Almost blinded by the brightness he brushed his hand against a cholla cactus and came away with one of the needles stuck in his hand. He didn't have anything to pull it out with, so he crawled on.

—⚉—

It seemed like days, but from how little the sun moved he knew it had been no longer than four of five hours. The ravine offered no solace, but he could go no further. He closed his eyes.

He heard a familiar voice. "You got away, too?"

Shielding his eyes with his one good hand, Darling saw the big man, Badger, standing over him. Badger was smiling and looked as big as ever. Darling tucked his fears of death aside and forced a grimaced smile. His words took forever to come out, but he heard himself speak, as if his thoughts were not parched to the extent of his mouth and tongue. "Badger." He tried some humor. "What took you so long?"

"They was something, eh?" Badger's face drawn tight, as cool as Darling had ever seen him, not a bead of sweat or hint of sunburn on his massive face.

"Water."

"Don't got water. But the mountains is closer than you think. Look." Badger gestured with his head, and Darling looked behind him. The mountains didn't seem far off. He might be able to make it. The big man could carry him.

"How'd you?" Then it hit him. Badger was standing directly over him in full daylight. There should be shade from his shadow. There was no shadow. There was no shade. Badger never got away.

"Those demons hurt me like hell." Badger's voice carried on the wind, fading, like he was walking away. "I think they had it in for us, like Carlos said. The boys gave them a fight, though." Darling's eyes must have closed, for when he opened them, Badger was gone.

Darling moved. The stench of death followed him, and he suspected it was the wounds from the creature's talons going gangrene. No death angels, owl demons, scalped avenging ghosts were going to get him. Didn't he kill one with a knife? Didn't Badger just say the others put up a helluva fight? Thorn in his hand or not, he could throttle the things with his bare hands, still. *They can't get me so easy. All I need is a touch of shade.*

Ahead he saw a lone mesquite tree in a wash. Shade. He scratched his way slowly, painfully toward it. Wait out the day in shade, move to the mountains at night.

He reached the tip of the shaded spot, his good hand in the coolness. Immediately an intense sting and pressure bit into the hand, as if he had grabbed hold of an active hornet's nest. He rolled on his back in time to see the upside-down image of a young rattler slithering away in the dust.

The pain gave way to a spreading numbness. He pushed away from the shade into the direct sun, instinctively trying to get as far from the rattler as possible. *Damn you*, he thought. *Damn all of you. I'm going to make it no matter what you throw at me.* He tried to laugh but managed a knotty cough instead. *Well, I can die before the demons get at me. That will show the sons of bitches.*

Already his jaw was numb as the poison coursed through his system. Then the numbness was replaced with fire, as his blood became more like a habanero pepper sauce. Then everything was numb again. He could go no further. All that was moving were his thoughts. *I did bad things. But, no matter. It's a bad world, and I ain't got worse coming to me than anybody I hurt or kilt.*

A wisp of shade drifted over his slit-opened eyes. It lingered a second then was gone. Relief. Anything to stop the killing sun. Waves of shade washed over him, over and over. He felt the momentary coolness each time, the interrupted brutality of the sun. Shade. Shade spread over him. Whatever had cast the long shadows that bathed his body was beside him, and by the rippling darkness, over him as well. With one eye he saw high in the sky a buzzard swooping in a gentle arc, spiraling downward. Then another. And another.

With what little mouth he had left he smiled. *Buzzards*, he thought. *Just buzzards. A touch of shade.*

There was no numbness or lack of silent screaming when the first of the buzzards dipped its beak into his already putrefying abdomen.

I've always liked reading and watching Westerns, and I am a big fan of Elmore Leonard, Larry McMurtry, Charles Portis, Cormac McCarthy, Louis L'Amour, and many others. I enjoy writing stories that take place in an earlier time, especially those in the 19th and early 20th centuries. The research is fun, even though I worry that I don't always get it right when I'm working on the story. Nothing turns me off faster than when I'm reading someone else's work, particularly historical fiction, and I notice that a gun used didn't exist at the time the story takes place, or something that shows the writer didn't take the time to do research. Still, mistakes happen, and it is fiction, after all.

"A Touch of Shade" was inspired in part by Cormac McCarthy's Blood Meridian, *one of the finest horror stories ever written, in my opinion. Once I had the basic idea of a marauding band of scalp hunters getting their comeuppance, the story practically wrote itself.*

Not Buried Deep Enough

Originally published in The Horror Zine, *2018*

A scratch at the door. She shoots the son of a bitch dead, in the head and chest. Drags the body by the legs, grabbing there just above the muddy boots so they don't slide off, drags the body to the porch and down the steps.

She takes a break. Smokes a cigarette. The wind lifts the smoke to the clouds and beyond, and the humidity is godawful. Relaxed, sitting on his dead rump, drawing her knees up and sucking the smoke into her lungs, holding and exhaling. Just relaxing. Two stars, three, popping out. Nobody's business.

It smells like rain. Weatherman said a slight chance before she blew the television to smithereens. Henry's ass is rock hard. She flicks the cigarette matching the lightning bugs. They are all in love.

She got him, this time. Stopped him short at the back door, surprised him with his own .357, couldn't miss so close even with the black strings that could be shadows, could be anything but the light of day. The never-easy tall man wearing shadows like his flannel shirt, and rotten off the bone blue jeans more a filthy green, who knows what snot he rolled in before he got here. The man deserved to die. Again, and again, and again.

Bonnie lifts her head looking above the house, not direct, not looking at anything anymore. A breeze lifts strands of hair off her nose and across her forehead, back where they belong. He was a mess. Coming after her the way he did. Always something.

Once upon a time she is oblivious, in the kitchen. He loves her chili.

So, she makes chili. He is far away, will never smell her chili again. She makes it for herself. Browns the ground beef and pork. Drains all but two tablespoons of fat. Add garlic and onion, cook and stir until tender.

He lunges out of the wall, the blade slicing neat holes.

Add tomato sauce, water, beer, chili powder, bouillon, cumin, paprika, oregano…sugar. Do I even know you, yes, I've seen your face, your diabolical round eyes, your straight line red mouth, colander, yes, cocoa, hot sauce. Mix well. Falling against the floor fighting for her life. Her life. She hears the blade enter her, doesn't feel it, hears the tearing, like cloth. Think. Boil. Reduce. Simmer.

She is out in the country, but she hears city sounds. Horns. Shouts. Babies wailing. Children screeching. Drunkards cursing. Laughter. The falling stink of the city curtains, no small bowl, this. Stirring cornmeal, flour, warm water. Warm water flowing out of her.

Not again. She drags the body across the dirt and high grass of an unkempt lawn. To the edge of a woods. Leaves the body there in a soft blanket of dark where the stars can't reach, ever, runs back to the house to the garage and grabs an old rusty shovel.

Stir the meat into the chili and cook, covered, an additional twenty minutes. Roll back white eyes.

With the shovel she breaks ground. My name is Bonnie, she says to herself. But Mary is there with her, Elizabeth, too. Annie is behind them saying soft things tinged with hate. We are Bonnie. We are broken. The warm Texas night syrup, dark and delicious. She knows this scene oh too well. Horse hooves clattering on brick, footsteps, millions of footsteps, voices intermingled as one, loud, harsh from lifted lights, worms working their way up, indeed, loosening the soil, helping her. Breaking her. Fog. Rich and accepting, sweepy fog.

She digs. The shovel is heavy, and the earth is hard in places, roots, she thinks, and she chops at it with all the strength she has left. Then on her knees, scraping with her hands, pushing dirt aside, sweat splattering off her or maybe a light rain now, the few stars gone. Catherine, someone says. An introduction she hears as clear as the wind rattling the branches nearby.

Voices, hands, many hands around her—she senses this because her eyes are closed, not wanting to see. The voices chatter in thick accents, and she can't decipher a word of it. But they are with her. They give her strength.

Deep enough. She rolls the body into the shallow pit. Handfuls of dirt, sprinkled like seasoning. Then she shovels the loose dirt onto the body and around the sides, patting it lightly with the backside of the shovel. It takes a long time, and the rain is stronger, tympanic against the leaves and grass. The voices are gone. They will be back.

Bonnie rubs her wet arms. Stretches. Walks back to the house and takes the shotgun resting on the kitchen table like a broken trail of smoke, brings it back to the fresh grave. She unloads two blasts into the soft mound of dirt. "Damn you, Henry," she says. *The flesh you break. I will* break *you*.

Stir the chili. Taste. Repeat. Saucy. Saucy Jack.

The lights are out. She sits at the table in the dark, waiting. There was a man, once, she knew. Tall and strong, he liked to hurt her in quiet, secret ways. She ran from him, but he always found her, no matter where or how far she went. She tries but can't picture his face. Could she ever picture it? What did he ever do to you, really? Mary asks. Or is it, Elizabeth? He grew old, Bonnie replies, scuttling about the kitchen.

The house is small, six rooms, a cabin miles from nowhere. There are trees everywhere that muffle sounds from the distant roads and neighbors. She paces each room patting the bloodstained walls, stepping over the remains of his dogs, remembers him at the bathroom sink in the morning gargling in such an irritating way, not knowing where he was or who he was.

The coffee is cold. But she empties the pot into flowery cups that are set on end tables, blanket chests, the fireplace mantle. In case her guests are thirsty.

She caught him by surprise in the morning, caught him before he caught her. Oh, she knew who he was, a hundred years removed, and her friends laughed that she used a knife, at first. The dogs barked like crazy. Didn't like her dragging him out, holding on to him with their teeth until she took care of them, too. She put him in a shallow hole where a garden might someday be.

He came back. Surprised her in the living room, coming up behind her, and if it wasn't for the shrieks of Catherine and Elizabeth…well, he was old and dead, moving so slow she was able to hit him in the head with the fireplace poker. She let him lay there for a while to catch her breath, then grabbed him by the feet and pulled him back out to the fresh dug-up spot and put him back. She was drenched with sweat. The house was hot with the windows closed, but she had to keep them that way. There were enough flies in the place as it was. And she didn't want him trying to climb through the open windows.

All day long she kills him, the empty-eyed monster. She has buried him too many times to remember. There are fresh mounds all over the yard. The voices worn on her like a tight-fitting wool cap. And the heat is so damn oppressive. Why does she have to make chili, on all days when it is so hot?

His favorite dish. All those years sitting next to him, sitting across from him, lying in the same bed but never once really touching, not knowing the secrets hidden in that black mind of his.

The wood floor is slick. Henry's gray hair abuzz to the empty space leading to the hall. She fires three shots into the space blasting bits of plaster and wood where he once was. She takes one of his knives and scratches it along the wall until it reaches a painting of a smoking city, rips through the buildings and chimneys and blue clouds. All the blue clouds.

Stay down, Henry, she says.

Bonnie locks the door, checks it a minute later to be sure. Locked. Unlocked. Locked. She can't remember. She is bone tired. There was a man once. Henry. Not his real name. There was a man once…

She prays it is over this time. Closes her eyes and voices scream in her head. *We hope he is in the ground for good. We hope.*

The man has been killed a thousand times in her head. Over the years she has stabbed him, set him on fire, shot him with practically every handgun and rifle the man owned. Henry has a crossbow. She used to picture the arrow clean through his evil heart. Thirty-something years together, and it was the only thing that made her smile.

The voices convinced her who he really was. The soul survives and moves on, and even though he petted the dog and never took a hand to her she knew—*she knew*—what was lurking beneath. Everything made sense then, why she hated him the way she did, why the very picture of him in her mind made her sick. It was only a matter of time before he let loose on her the way he did those unfortunate women in London.

I did this for you, she says. Turning this way and that. It is so hot to be cooking. The pores of her skin are steaming, and her black dyed hair is coiled wet like a medusa dream. She whimpers running through the house, spinning and dropping to her knees to pray and look for the crossbow under the bed. Not there, she shoves the hallway closet door open and rummages past shoes and stacked boxes, jackets, and wrinkled coats, listens to make sure he isn't working to get in the house again. What did he do with it, and how do you use it anyway?

Plug an arrow in and shoot at the target. Simple. Got to find it. Used up all the bullets, glancing at pockmarked walls and ceilings.

It occurs to her to just leave this place, the man in the ground. Leave everything behind. But she can't do it. Voices brought her here, voices keep her here. Mary, Elizabeth, Annie, Catherine. She hears fresh voices soft and delicate, feathers of death. She looks at the raw and broken blisters on her dirty hands, the dried blood, his and hers, on her blouse and pants.

So much to do…

The chili is on the stove. She has bowls out on the table now. The guests will be hungry. She hears their voices, knows they are still around. The man in the shallow grave stirs and whispers and shrugs against the soft earth while the voices strong drown his cries outside.

Outside.

Staring at the empty bowls and the empty shotgun and the empty pistol, what did she do with the shovel dragging her legs under her on the chair in the dismal light. Doesn't matter where she is, farm out in the country or loud fog shrouded city with broken lights and cobbled stones and dreams.

There is a scratch at the door. She is sure it is him. Dead sure.

This story was meant to be experimental in form, likely inspired by some of the beat writers like William S. Burroughs and Charles Bukowski.

The germ of an idea for the story came from an experience I had back in the early eighties, when I was living in an upstairs apartment in a two-family house. The landlady and owner, the grandmother of one of my best friends, lived in the lower apartment. She had been ill for some time and was beginning to show signs of dementia. Her family asked me to check in on her when I could. One day I knocked, and she invited me into her smoke-filled apartment. There was a party going on, only there were no people.

Ashtrays, some with smoldering cigarettes, were everywhere, as well as glasses of beer, liquor, and soda, some full, some half-full, some almost empty. Plates of food were on the table and coffee table and on the armrests of the chair and couch. The television was on with the volume turned up loud. She explained to me that everyone had just left, then told me names of guests who had been there—mostly old friends and family members.

I helped her clean up, then after I went upstairs, I called her daughter (my friend's mother) and explained what had happened. I mentioned most of the names I could remember. The daughter was shocked—all the names were of relatives or friends who had been dead for some time. We were both unsettled by the lit cigarettes and the mess of a party that wasn't a party, but most of all we were unsettled by the grandmother being visited by her long-lost loved ones. The grandmother suffered a stroke a few days later and died several days after that.

I tried for years to put that experience into a story. "Not Buried Deep Enough" was as close as I got. There are references to Jack the Ripper and his victims, and I wanted it ambiguous as to whether Bonnie was truly insane or if she was dealing with a reincarnated horror.

The Holes We Become

Baxter hammered the FOR SALE sign into the rain-softened ground. The neighbor across the street stood in her doorway and watched as he straightened the sign. Baxter noticed another neighbor a few houses down, standing in his yard, also watching what the real estate agent was doing. Baxter stepped back and admired his work and the nondescript 1978 two-story Colonial behind the sign, white siding and rust-colored brick, windows reflecting the setting sun and causing him to squint as he raised his head toward the black shingled roof.

It was an ordinary house in an ordinary neighborhood. And Baxter didn't think he would have any trouble selling it at the reduced price, regardless of the unfortunate events that befell the previous occupants.

—⁂—

Jules and Fiona Ramsey fell in love with the place—and the price—and didn't hesitate to make an offer. They made a ridiculously low offer. It was accepted without any haggling.

Jules and Fiona and their two children moved in two weeks later. A handful of items were left over from the estate sale and remained in the house: two bookcases, an antique pie safe, a dresser, a few small tables, an oriental rug in the foyer that still seemed in good shape, a few cheap farm scene paintings left hanging on the wall. Fiona put the paintings in the trash and kept everything else.

Of course, Ron Baxter, the agent, told them about the mysterious disappearance of the home's previous owners, the Willoughbys. "No one knows where they went," he said, as he took Jules and Fiona through the house.

"An entire family? Just up and left without a trace?" Jules was skeptical, by nature. He was a data scientist, and he read his fair share of horror and crime novels. The Willoughbys simply vanished, apparently while they were in the middle of eating dinner. John and Carol Willoughby, their three children, ages seven, nine, and thirteen. Whatever happened to them, there was no evidence of foul play and no indication they took anything with them—the car was in the garage, no clothes appeared to be missing, and John's wallet was on the kitchen counter along with Carol's purse containing her wallet and cell phone. Money, credit cards, and licenses were still there.

A neighbor called the police when no one answered the door or returned his calls, suspicious after seeing no activity for several weeks. When the police eventually entered the house, the television was on. The kitchen stank of rotting food. And the Willoughbys were gone.

The house was put on the market two years later by surviving family members. The mystery was a big deal in the local news for Denver and was mentioned in the national news. Investigators turned up nothing.

"Sounds like the Mary Celeste," Fiona said.

Baxter laughed. "Big difference between a ship deserted at sea and a house in a quiet neighborhood. My theory is that they simply took the kids and left—really left—went someplace for a fresh start with no ties to their former life. Maybe they were in the witness protection program and had to leave in a hurry." He saw the look of concern on Fiona's face. "It's safe here. No one would mistake you guys for the Willoughbys. Besides, it's been well over two years. And it's a great house at a great price."

—∞—

The unpacking finished for the day, Jules and Fiona sat in folding chairs in the backyard drinking wine and admiring the small patch of woods that pressed against the fence.

Squirrels chattered and nervously scrambled across branches of trees, while birds of all kinds disturbed the remaining brown and yellow leaves. "It's idyllic," Jules said.

"I should check on the children," Fiona said.

"They're fine. Let them explore their new kingdom."

"Hard to believe we have our own home. So peaceful." Fiona brushed her hair back and took another sip of wine. They could easily finish this bottle before going back inside, it was so tasty and relaxing. She didn't worry much about the kids, really. They were eight and six, and Jules was right, they could explore the house without causing any trouble. It's part of the fun of being a kid, right?

—⁂—

"You see that?' Will asked. He held the closet door open wide for Becky to see what was inside. Becky stood by her older brother. A shadow against the wall, the light at their backs, the shadow unmistakably that of Will.

Only it wasn't. When he stepped away from the door, off to the side in the room, the light from the bedroom window still at his back, the shadow should have disappeared, or at least moved.

It didn't.

The shadow, a likeness of Will, black and deep-looking, like a cut out in the wall, remained. Right next to Becky's shadow. In the closet. Becky giggled. This was a neat trick.

Will moved next to Becky, the black outline of his body frozen on the wall. The light was starting to fade as the sun set, but the shadow was still there even as Becky's shadow became less distinct and then disappeared altogether. The black image, as if painted on the wall, stayed, even as the growing darkness mixed with everything else.

Will was speechless. He couldn't take his eyes off it, this black hole cut in the wall in his shape. The shadow had depth, like he could walk up and squeeze into it.

Becky touched it, tried to, her hand disappearing into the black void. She screeched, jerked her hand out, backed up to the middle of the room well behind Will. "It's cold."

It was a hole. Where there had been nothing earlier in the day. Will wondered if Dad had cut it, some kind of weird joke.

If there was a hole, it should lead to Mom and Dad's room. This led to blackness. And Becky said it was cold. Will couldn't turn away from it. It was his shape. His hole. He had to see if he could fit into it. Becky said something, maybe she was running from the room. Didn't matter. "I'm going to see what this is," he said to himself.

As he moved toward it, arms outstretched, the hole wiggled and shifted, like a mirage. He squeezed his eyes shut and opened them. The hole was gone.

—⁂—

"Look at this," Jules said. He turned the laptop enough for Fiona to see the screen. He had Googled the address, pulled up information on all the past owners, all the way back to when the house was built, 1964. The first owner was Charles Bertrand. Jules pointed to the name on the screen. "That name is familiar, somehow." He turned the laptop and typed away, while Fiona watched quietly, sipping from her glass of wine. "Wow." His eyes widened.

"Well?" Fiona said it dead-tone, like she could care less to know anything about any of the previous owners, except perhaps the most recent ones. The ones who disappeared.

Jules sat back on the couch, and again turned the screen to face Fiona. She squinted and tried to read, and since he knew she didn't have her reading glasses, he went ahead and explained. "Charles Bertrand. The son of a bitch was known as the Cherry Creek butcher. Killed eight people that they know of, probably many more. I remember something about that, even though it was long before our time."

Suddenly Fiona was interested. "Here? Our house?"

"No. He didn't do anything here, as far as I know. In fact, it says he was a respected member of the community, an engineer, had a wife and several kids. Family man by day, vicious killer by night. No one suspected a thing. Which I find hard to believe…"

"How'd they catch him, then?"

Jules read quietly for a minute. "Apparently, someone saw a man lurking around Cherry Creek in the vicinity of one of the murders and was able to give a description. It took the police a year to eventually nail him, but they did. The man kept trophies of his victims. Those they found here. In this house. In the basement. Fuck."

"I don't like that. It's too creepy. If I had known…"

"Aren't they supposed to disclose shit like that? Damn."

Fiona breathed like she was trying to suck all the air from the room. "At least it was a long time ago. It doesn't make me feel much better."

Jules continued to scroll and silently read. "Get this. Bertrand's wife and two kids disappeared after he was convicted. No one knows where they went or what became of them."

"Could you blame them?"

"No, I mean, they just up and left, didn't put the house up for sale or anything. They were here one day, gone the next. Sound familiar?" Jules furiously typed on the keyboard.

Fiona stared over his head, looking at a spot on the wall by the fireplace she had missed. A smudge of ash or dirt, perhaps. Or a hole.

"Here," Jules said. "The next owners lived here for six years. The ones after that, let's see, twelve years. Don't know anything about them, at least nothing stands out. Nothing odd."

"Look up their names, see if anything comes up."

"Nothing. Looks like the house turned over a lot. Kind of unusual, but if people got wind of the history of the place, they could've freaked and moved out. Then we come to the Willoughbys." He paused. "You're not upset, are you?"

Fiona shook her head no. But the way she avoided looking in his eyes said, yes, she was unsettled by all of this. A lot.

—∞—

Becky rushed down the steps and ran into the living room. "Mom! Dad!" Fiona and Jules both jumped from the couch as if the house was on fire.

"What is it sweetie?" Fiona asked. Always calm, reassuring.

"There's someone in the wall!"

"What?" Fiona and Jules said at the same time.

"I heard someone crying. I think it's a girl, but I'm not sure."

Jules smiled and nodded his head. "You were dreaming, that's all. You must've heard me and Mom talking."

"It's funny how sounds and voices carry in a house, and if you were asleep…" Fiona gently nudged Becky's arm to start her back up the steps. They would all go up together.

"I wasn't asleep. And it wasn't your voices. It was someone crying. They're in my *wall*."

They were moving up the steps, Becky in the lead. "Could be," Jules said to Fiona, "an animal scurrying around in the walls. Maybe a mouse squeaking or a squirrel."

"Oh, my God," Fiona said. "I hate rats!"

"Shhh," Becky said as they entered her room. It was dead quiet.

Jules put his ear to the wall, Becky pointing to the spot where she heard the crying. She and Fiona stood back by Becky's bed, afraid something furry was going to jump through the wall.

Nothing did.

"I don't hear anything," Jules said. He tapped the wall. "If we had a little critter in here, it's gone now." He tried for a Walter Brennan voice, getting a chuckle for the dead actor out of Fiona.

"I heard it," Becky said. "Someone was crying in there."

—∞—

The next few days were quiet ones. Fiona and Jules couldn't get over how boxes of stuff seemed to mysteriously procreate and produce offspring. It was a running joke with the whole family. The house was bigger than anything they had ever lived in before, and every nook and cranny had to be explored. Becky didn't hear the crying again.

The basement was unfinished, gray concrete walls and floor, the furnace, a sink, an old washer and dryer. The basement gave Jules and Fiona the creeps, especially after knowing the history of the place, and Will and Becky avoided it unless they were with one of their parents. Jules wondered where Bertrand kept his souvenirs. He searched the walls and floor for secret panels or patched holes. He found nothing, of course.

Still, he was drawn to the basement when Fiona and the kids weren't around. To look. There was always that chance he had missed something, some clue, something that was a tie-in with Charles Bertrand. The Cherry Creek Butcher.

And, somehow, somewhere, there had to be a connection between Bertrand's family and the Willoughby family. He was determined to find it.

—⁂—

"Something touched the back of my neck," Fiona told Jules. She had rushed up the steps when she realized it wasn't a spider or a bug, and when she further realized it was the touch from a finger. A cold finger.

Jules shook his head, smiling. Funny how the imagination works, that smile conveyed.

She had a deep bruise at the base of her neck, purple-green. The imprint of a finger, as if she had been poked hard. She couldn't have done it herself.

"Damn. That's pretty nasty," he said, now concerned.

She held a hand mirror and noticed it in the bathroom mirror. It itched like crazy. "I felt a gentle poke. Like someone trying to get my attention. And it was freezing."

She looked at Jules. "This place isn't right."

—⁂—

He really liked this place. And now Fiona and Becky having second thoughts. Hell. He was getting a kick out of this, living in a place with a notorious reputation, a rich history, and the way his neighbors looked at him and held their thoughts and their words. All because of where he lived. Jules didn't believe in ghosts, or the boogieman, or dark angels, none of that crap. He believed in hard science. And quiet, serene surroundings. And a house that he actually owned.

No fucking way was he going to pack up and retreat. No way he was going back to an apartment or condo. He was very sorry he mentioned anything about the Cherry Creek Butcher to Fiona in the first place. This house, for now anyway, was a perfect fit for him.

Everyone else was going to have to find a way to fit in, too.

The thoughts, and the wine, in his head. That was when he heard the screams. Becky. Again.

He ran into the house. Fiona was already rushing up the stairs. Becky was in Will's room, screaming hysterically. The screams crackling and increasing in pitch until only a squeak, like air squeezed from a balloon, remained when Fiona and Jules ran into the room.

Becky stood frozen, staring into the bare closet. No sound came from her mouth. She didn't turn her head when her parents barged into the room, breathless.

"Becky, what's wrong?" Fiona asked, kneeling beside her.

Becky, mute, pointed into the closet.

"Where's your brother?" Jules asked. Becky continued to point to the closet.

"Becky!" Fiona turned Becky's head with her index finger. *C'mon, look at me.*

Becky sniffled, on the verge of a meltdown. "Will walked into the shadow."

"What are you talking about?" Jules said.

"Will!" Becky shouted.

Jules looked toward the doorway expecting his son to come in from the hall.

"He's in there," Becky said. The closet was clearly empty, except for a few small boxes. Nothing had been hung up yet on the wooden rod. There was a dark outline, like a faint stain, but dark enough to take on the appearance of a shadow. "He went into the hole. Then the hole went away."

"What hole, darling?" Fiona turned her head to the hallway door. "Will, get in here!"

"I'll check and see where he is," Jules said.

"Maybe he went into the basement."

"He went into the hole," Becky said. "He fit into it like a piece of puzzle."

"I'm sure Will's just exploring the house. He wouldn't go into any hole, and besides, there is no hole in there. See?" Jules patted the inside closet walls. Solid taps. "Maybe he was messing with you. Hiding somewhere."

"Go check, will you?" Fiona was unsettled enough.

Jules checked all the rooms upstairs. And the closets. He called Will's name over and over. He threatened that if this was a game, he better come out from hiding now or he was going to be in deep trouble. He went down the stairs, each step feeling spongy, as if his feet sank slightly in the wood. *Nerves*, he thought.

He was getting worried. He heard Fiona lead Becky back to her room. Every light upstairs clicked on as he made his way to the main level. He turned on every light. Will could be outside. No, it was too late. He wouldn't go out this time of night. And certainly not without permission.

The basement. He flipped the light switch at the top of the stairs. All the other lights in the basement had to be turned on by pulling a string, the old-fashioned way. He checked beneath the stairs, a good place to hide. Nothing except a few dried-out paint cans. The anger was building in him. He didn't know what he might do when he found Will.

He walked into the center of the basement and pulled the string to a lone 40-watt bulb. The damp musty odor of an old basement was never stronger than it was now. He wondered if there were multiple leaks that were never disclosed. He looked behind the furnace and the water heater. Something caught his eye on the far wall next to an empty metal shelf. A dark spot, a *large* dark spot. *There it is*, he thought, *the fucking water damage*. The stain seeming to grow larger as he watched.

Jules pulled another string to another light as he approached it. The bulb didn't work.

Burnt out. But he could see clear enough, the stain standing out on the dull yellow paint. The stain seemed black in this light and appeared to have depth to it. *And, damn*, Jules thought, *might be mold, the deepest darkest mold I've ever seen.* He didn't want to touch it, but he brought his hand close to it, waved over it, felt a coolness. *A leak, somewhere.*

The stain was his height. Interesting. He couldn't take his eyes off it. Will had already receded far back in his mind, and the calls from Fiona upstairs grew steadily distant as he moved closer to the stain. The world began here. Everything else was a distraction.

This was maybe where the Cherry Creek Butcher kept his souvenirs, this black spot, which, as he was drawn closer, was a *hole*.

In the shape of a shadow. *His* shadow.

Now close enough to put his nose into the hole, this cool blackness, a feeling of nostalgia, a longing for something he couldn't define, came over him. He wanted things to be undone. Everything. And then, slipping into his consciousness, fear, wet and unrelenting fear. It paralyzed him. And he couldn't even begin to know where this fear came from.

It wasn't the shadow shape that was a replica of him, legs slightly apart, arms out from the sides, head tilted, a crucifix image on the wall, an opening. A doorway. *His doorway.*

Curiosity drove him. It was his shape, after all, and he wanted to press against it and into it. The thought of mold, or any apprehensive thought about the thing in front of him, vanished. With his arms outstretched he shuffled to it and pressed into the hole, felt himself sinking through the wall. Like Becky said, a puzzle piece. A perfect fit.

—⁓—

Jules wasn't answering her calls now, either. Did he find Will, and they were playing games with her and Becky? Fiona was worried but pissed, too. If Jules could only have kept his mouth shut about the house's sordid history…

She knew Becky didn't want to be left alone. "C'mon," Fiona said, "let's go downstairs and see what's taking Dad so long."

Becky took her hand, and they went down to the main level. Every light was on, every door closed, and the only sounds were their rhythmic breathing and muted heartbeats.

"Mom, I'm scared."

The game, if it was one, was way out of control. Fiona opened the door to the basement and said, "Jules? Will?"

Fuck Jules, she thought. She was fucking tired of his games. His know-it-all, condescending attitudes, his *infidelity*. He thought he was so slick. So superior. He never suspected that she knew all about Rena, their little office affair, had known for over a month now. At first, she didn't know how she knew, it was just a feeling, a gut-wrenching suspicion connected to his odd work hours and the boring details of his job he was always bringing up. A cover.

His eyes flickered secretly sometimes when he received texts at all hours of the day or night, and sometimes people just know when someone they love is betraying them. Cautious. Deliberate. Secretive. And when she met Rena once, running into her at T.G.I. Fridays, the way Jules and Rena looked at each other—and didn't look at each other—as introductions were made, and the awkward brief chatter that followed. The way it had been between them in the bedroom, everywhere really, an invisible cold wall that you could talk over but not get through.

Fuck Jules.

Holding hands, Fiona and Becky moved painstakingly slow down the steps, looking for anything out of the ordinary. Two of the lights were already on but the one by the furnace was out. That part of the basement darker, a shadow sense of the well-lit areas. A place hiding secrets.

The basement was warm. And damp. Fiona could smell the dampness, the humidity thick in the air like a swamp summer evening. The concrete floor along the base of the far wall appeared wet. Fiona pulled the string to the light by the furnace, but it didn't come on. She reached up and twisted the bulb. Still nothing. No mistaking the dark patch along the wall. Water was getting through the foundation. Jules had done a top-notch job inspecting this place before they bought it. Asshole.

"Let's go upstairs, sweetie. They're not down here," Fiona said. They went up the stairs, Becky silent, loosely holding Fiona's hand the whole time. "They must be outside." Jules obviously went out to look for Will. Fiona was still pissed, and she couldn't figure out why. And those thoughts about Jules having an affair. Where did that come from? And where did she get that name? Rena.

They had never been to a T.G.I. Fridays in Denver. Her imagination was on fire.

They stood in the center of the kitchen, next to the table. Fiona didn't know which way to go, back upstairs or into the living room, or should she take Becky with her outside? She was stuck. Something was wrong about everything. Her memory. Her emotions. The fear that was building from someplace deep within her. She could have been Becky's age, the way she felt, alone and not knowing anything. She was broken, and she didn't want to be broken.

"Mom." Becky pointed to the floor in front of the refrigerator. A stain spread from beneath the refrigerator, a large stain. They hadn't seen it earlier when they walked through the kitchen. The dark spot, like a huge colony of tiny black ants, spread out in the likeness of a woman's body.

"What the hell?" Fiona went over to it and leaned down to get a better look. It *did* seem alive. And deep. It mesmerized her, the way it vibrated and grew.

Becky tugged at her hand. Fiona's eyes locked on the black mass. Somehow, she thought of the beach, dark clouds competing against the sun, a long shadow drifting over the sand and over her and Roger, her first love, next to her, also getting swallowed by the soothing cool shadow. Roger. She had spurned him for Jules, so long ago, and she missed him, really missed him. She knew that now. Fiona stepped into the boiling shadow that was deep as all eternity, without thinking, without feeling the little hand frantically squeezing before letting go. Letting go.

She turned and looked at Becky, not knowing who this little girl was, then looked at the hole she was sinking into, a hole that was shaped like her, like it was meant just for her. Fiona bent her knees and spread her arms out and leaned forward into the hole, dipping her head as if she was diving into a black pool of water. She dove.

—⁓—

Becky screamed. She was all alone now. She screamed and screamed, but the screams didn't go anywhere. She ran to the front door. Had to get outside. Had to get help. But she tripped over the rug in the entryway and fell headfirst against the hard wooden floor. Shadow figures were everywhere—on the wall, on the floor, even on the ceiling, coming through, she was sure, from the rooms above her. The shadow figures were holes, unmoving, and of all sizes. They reminded her of pattern holes left behind from cut out paper dolls.

She crawled and scrambled to the door. She couldn't open it. She closed her eyes and opened them again. The holes were still there. And there was something else. Faintly, like a radio left on in a faraway room, she heard voices, many voices, and mixed in with the voices, laughter and crying. Distant sounds coming out of every human-shaped hole.

Becky was scared, but more overpowering was a sense of loneliness. She had never felt so alone, so abandoned.

Every morning she'd woken before the others and lay in bed, the covers pulled up over her mouth, and she listened for any sound that betrayed the existence of others in the house. She often heard Will toss and turn in the moments before he awoke. Or heard Mom and Dad moving about in their room, or, if it was later, water running in the kitchen and mumbled, half-asleep conversation. But sometimes it was dead quiet, and she could not hear a thing, and those were the worst moments, because that was when she realized she might be alone, abandoned. Left in the new house by herself. And the fear would swallow her until there was some sign that someone was in the house with her.

This was like that, only she wasn't in her bed safe under the covers. And she had seen Will disappear into a hole that seemed designed for him. And Mom disappear into a hole designed for her. She assumed Dad disappeared the same way.

This was different, though. Holes were everywhere. All sizes. All shaped like people. Shadow-people doors that led…where? No place that could be good. But where was her shadow? Her hole? Why was she left behind? She wanted to be with Will and Mom and Dad. She strained to hear their familiar voices amid the cacophony of mumbled noise.

"Mom! Dad!" Faint, indistinct voices came from each hole along with faraway cries, shouts, shrieks, fading screams. She went from hole to hole, listening, but the closer her ear was to the black abyss, the further the voices, the further the sounds. She reached into each hole and her arm would disappear into black mist. Sometimes the holes were freezing. Sometimes warm and soothing. She wondered how deep they were. She was so small. If she squeezed into one of the holes all the way, or fell into one...

With each dark shape she reached her hand into something came over her, a feeling she could go no further. The holes were not meant for her. And when she put her head in one, all smell, hearing, taste, sight, and touch disappeared, everything black and empty, and even thoughts left until she found herself outside, on the lawn, in the early morning. A woman she didn't know or recognize standing over her asking if she was okay, what was wrong, where were her parents?

Everything swept into Becky at once. The sight of clouds spinning from the old woman's head into a pink sky, cars rumbling on the street, children, faraway, screeching and laughing, the smell of wet grass and the lady's perfume, the taste of dirt on her fingers and lips.

She looked at the house and didn't recognize a thing. She didn't know why she was outside. She didn't know who she was or who she belonged to. She was empty and she knew she was empty, and she was sad, even though she didn't know why she was sad. She opened her mouth to speak, but only grunts and squeals came out. The lady kept asking questions she didn't understand. She stared at nothing and shook her head.

In time the police came. There was a great deal of hustle and noise, people everywhere, and she was taken away in a car with a blanket wrapped around her. She heard birds and sirens, and much later, in dreams and memory teases, screams.

—⁓—

Months later, Baxter, the real estate agent, hammered a FOR SALE into the soft ground. The neighbors gathered on their lawns and porches and watched in silence as he did his duty. Some shook their heads, and some wondered to themselves whatever happened to the little girl with the golden hair who was never able to speak or provide any clue about what happened to the rest of her family. The girl was taken away, and no one ever heard of what became of her. Such a shame.

When Baxter was done, he stood back from the sign and briefly looked at the house. It was a nice-looking place. He shook his head. *Unbelievable, all the bad luck. Maybe the next owners will scrape it and build something new.*

"The Holes We Become" was inspired by a short manga story by Junji Ito, titled "The Enigma of Amigara Fault." It's a terrifying story where people are

drawn to holes shaped just like them, and then after fitting into the holes they reemerge somewhere else as misshapen hideous beings.

I wanted to write another haunted house story incorporating some elements from Ito's story, and to leave the reader with the uncomforting notion that, even if the house was destroyed, the "holes" would remain.

The mission of Denver Horror Collective is to facilitate, celebrate, and inspire horror writers and artists throughout Colorado.

To be kept abreast of the Centennial State's literary horror scene go to denverhorror.com to join as a member and/or subscribe to our monthly e-newsletter, *The Epitaph*.

You can also follow Denver Horror Collective:

Facebook / Meta
(@denverhorror)

twitter
(@denver_horror)

TikTok
(DenverHorrorCollective)

Instagram
(@denver_horror)

YouTube
(@denverhorrorcollective)

Darkest Wishes,
Denver Horror Collective

Milton Keynes UK
Ingram Content Group UK Ltd.
UKHW010722110124
435856UK00001B/78